VOICE INSIDE

VOICE INSIDE

ARIES ZENREAL

TABLE OF CONTENTS

TWO ROOM SCHOOL...1
TRAUMA CARE...5
TWENTY YEARS LATER...10
FAMILY AFFAIR..14
THREE YEARS LATER..17
BABY BROTHERS..20
THREE YEARS LATER..26
DR. PERCY..29
RAIMEE...34
MARY LOSES IT..37
MEETING ONE-GROUP..40
TWO-FACED..45
FAMILY TIME..47
PROFESSIONAL RAIMEE..53
MARY'S NIGHT...56
MEETING TWO-GROUP..63
FLASHBACK..68
FRIENDS..69
ORGANIZATION...82
CONFESSIONS..85
DOCTOR CONSULT...89
MIDWEST..95
REFERRAL..109
EMPLOYER LOYALTY..113
CANADA BOUND..117
BYE CANADA BYE..133
REVELATIONS...139
MARY'S REVEAL...152
THE CAFÉ..156
ZENITH TRIP...159
TERMS...163
ORIENTATION...168
DEBRIEF...174
A ZENITHIAN NIMI..177
EARTH DISASTERS...178
SEEKING LOVE..182

MATCHMAKER...189

MERIDIUS...191

ZENITHIAN ALLEGIANT WARRIORS.................................197

ROLES AND RESPONSIBILITIES.....................................208

ZAPP...212

GIFTS..220

RETURN EARTH..223

RELEASE THE GIFT..230

I'M HOME...232

TOGETHER AGAIN..237

CONTAGIOUS..239

QUARANTINE...241

MESSAGE WAITING..244

PERKS..249

APPEARANCES...253

AUTHOR BIO...257

TWO ROOM SCHOOL

The rural, slightly suburban neighborhood clad with houses of different sizes, shapes and conditions have plentiful home-ownership for all its diverse neighbors. It is a slow walk or a quick drive. Either way you travel, if you turn your head you might miss this oh so familiar place. If you say, you live in Dodge City everybody knows where you are from. Children play, adults walk, men, and women well in their upper seventies and early eighties and well known in the neighborhood hold it down and hustle to earn a living.

As in many neighborhoods, this one is no different with churches on every corner, Baptist, Jehovah Witness, Presbyterian, Catholic, Episcopal, Anglican, Apostolic, Methodist, Nazarene, Non Denominational, and many others ensure plenty of religious and spiritual meeting places.

With the many churches in one small community and churchgoers making up the congregations of various denominations there are still many who do not attend church. Many wonder why there are so many denominations.

"I still haven't figured it out."

∞

Situated between two apartment buildings sits a graying home; the yard is collection central. Adjacent is a one-story grade school. First grade is on one side and second grade on the other side.

Raimee Alexander, a second grader plays outside with the class during recess. Covering the playground many young kids actively play hide and go seek and run all over the grounds.

Sanondra Forte chases Tyrone Nielson. "I'm gonna beat you up," Sanondra says in a scary voice, as she pushes and taunts Tyrone.

"Why are you picking on me San? I haven't done anything to you," Tyrone's wispy voice responds.

His posture and demeanor are like a frail weakling.

I'm gonna tell the teacher if you don't stop."

"Tell," San continues. "You know I don't care; I'll beat her up too."

She scares Tyrone. Sanondra beats up teachers. He knows she means what she says. She is so mean, strong, and peers at everybody with hate in her eyes.

"I'm going to call your parents and let them know just how you've been acting," the teacher, Ms. Lauwren Redding sternly tells San.

Sanondra scowls. "You can call them if you want; call any of my family, they won't do anything. My sister will come and beat you up, and then my oldest sister will come and beat you up. If you tell my mom she will come here and kick your ass."

Ms. Redding cautiously eyes San. She heads back in the building and informs the kids, "You have ten more minutes to play."

Bradley Woodson and Raimee motion to each other, run, and jump on the swing set. There are only two swing seats for both first and second grades.

"I can go higher than you," Bradley yells.

Both start out about the same pace, but Bradley swings stronger and higher. Raimee rides back and forth on the big swing with steel posts. She stares straight ahead.

Bradley does not know she has a phobia of heights.

Raimee goes much higher, not due to her efforts.

"Who's pushing me?" she asks.

"It's me James Moore."

"I'm going higher than Bradley.

"Whoa, whoa! Wait you're pushing me too high," Raimee yells out to James.

She goes so high the old swing bounces.

James does not listen to her. She is begging him to stop pushing her so high; he keeps pushing and pushing.

∞

She goes to the highest with her long legs completely stretched out.
"James stop," as her soft voice cracks. "Please stop, I'm scared."
She loses her grip on the handles. Her small hands break loose from the heavy chain. From high up in the air, she falls out of the swing.
She falls to the ground.
BAM!
CLONK!
Her head hits extremely hard on the heavy-duty steel pole.
She lies motionless on the ground.

TRAUMA CARE

Tina is first to run toward her.

"Raimee are you okay?"

Raimee is not moving, she is not responding.

All the kids run to see what is happening. They are hovering over her.

"Ms. Redding, Ms. Redding, she hit her head and is not moving. Come outside quick."

"What's wrong? How did she hit her head?" Ms. Redding quickly runs outside, "Move out the way and let me look at her."

"She's knocked out cold Ms. Redding."

Ms. Redding bends over Raimee and gently places a cold cloth over her head. Her limp body does not move. She dials 911, and she calls Mr. and Mrs. Alexander, Raimee's parents.

∞

Mom and dad Alexander drive directly to Memoriam hospital arriving around the time paramedics unload her from the ambulance.

They take her to the back area of the emergency room.

"Take her to triage, room five," the nurse attendant quickly says.

Mrs. Alexander removes Raimee's clothes and drapes the hospital gown around her body.

The triage nurse walks in, "She will go for x-rays in about ten minutes."

About twenty minutes after the x-rays, the nurse returns, "Mr. and Mrs. Alexander, Raimee's x-rays have been taken, Dr. Kreason will review them, and as soon as he has an answer will let you know."

"Okay, but please let us know something as soon as possible. Please," Mr. Alexander politely asserts.

"Yes sir, we will."

Mr. Alexander nervously continues, "She's only seven years old. I just want her to be okay and not be crippled from this."

Mrs. Alexander paces the floor. "This waiting is getting to my nerves. I do not know how much longer I can wait to find out what is happening. The doctor needs to tell us something."

"Honey, give them time," Mr. Alexander calmly responds. "We want them to make the right decisions and try to give her the best care possible."

"Yeah," Mrs. Alexander blows out a long breath. It's not a sigh of relief; it's merely a sound of frustration oozing out of her anxious body.

Dr. Kreason enters the room. "The x-ray films show a concussion; it's all we know so far. We will admit her for additional monitoring and testing if necessary to make sure she'll be okay."

"Finally we receive some news. Her father will go home and get some clean clothes? I will be spending the night at the hospital.

"Are you going to stay?" she asks of her husband.

"Where will we both sleep? You know I have to be somewhat comfortable so I can go to work tomorrow. The only reason I am going to work is we need the money; my little girl means the world to me. I will be right back after work. Actually, I'll try to get off a little earlier."

"Okay, just get us something to sleep in, to change into tomorrow, and some toiletries. I will check with the nurse for another available fold out sleeping chair. Take your time and be careful. I need you here for the both of us."

∞

One-hour later attendants take Raimee to the third floor for night observation.

"I'm so happy they put you in a private room. This is the way your father and I can spend the night without bothering another patient. I can make the temperature in the room what we need it to be. It's freezing in here right now, so I'll turn the heat up a little for you baby."

"Where is daddy?" she groggily asks.

"He should be back from getting our things from home soon. It's about 8:00 p.m. and he will need to be sleep no later than 10:00 p.m. Mommy wants you to rest and don't worry about a thing."

The nurse walks in with a pressure cup in her hand. She softly asks, "How are you feeling? I need to get a blood pressure reading. Tell me how your head feels. Can I get you some water or soda?"

"Yes a little soda pop, please," she answers with a sleepy voice of pain. She slowly rubs her small hand across her forehead.

∞

"My head is really sore and hurts. Mommy, daddy, my head hurts," she cries.

Mrs. Alexander takes Raimee's hand and gently rubs it back and forth. She remarks, "You hit your head so hard you have a nasty concussion." While she anxiously presses the help buzzer, she states, "I'll get the nurse."

The nurse runs in the room; Raimee writhes in agony.

TWENTY YEARS LATER

Mary Sutton, twenty years old, lives at 33019 Crestmore Drive in a three bedroom, two-story house with her mom, Ms. Juanita Sutton and two younger brothers, Malcolm and Bobby.

She is playing cards with kids younger than she is. "Go ahead Mary, it's your turn. Can you Go Fish?" a kid holding cards asks.

Mary remarks, "I'm tired of playing this card game. Let's play something else. What about spades or rummy?"

Acting like the leader of the group, "These games are old and they're not fun now. Let's play another game; a game we like and want to play," Drema begs.

"Like what?" Mary asks. "Ya'll don't like Operation or Old Maid. What other games are there? Maybe you all can watch your older brothers and sisters play spades and rummy. What about your parents?

"Go ahead and play what you want. I'm tired anyway and I am going in the house. My mom won't care if you play on our porch. If I am better after I sleep for a little I might come back out and play again. See ya'll later."

"Mary I wish you would stay with us; you are fun. You can go in later and get some sleep," one kid says.

Mary with sleepy squinty eyes remarks, "I'll talk with ya'll later."

Still playing, the other kids respond to Mary's quick decision to quit,

"See you later."

"Bye Mary."

"See you tomorrow."

They walk down the street, glance at each other, and shrug their shoulders. Before you know it, the chase is on after each other. They laugh aloud. Mary becomes a distant past.

One kid checks her pockets, "I have some change; we can share a soda. What kind do you want me to buy, root beer, orange, or grape?"

∞

Mary relaxes on the living room couch. She does not want to go to sleep. She sits in front of the TV, remote in hand, ready to play a DVD. The movie turns out to be a DVD of a previous recorded group therapy session. Nine people, all inpatients at the New Hope Therapeutic Home are in a session. They sit in a circle and discuss issues bothering them.

∞

Rita Doverton quickly stands, looks around the room, and asks the question, "What is that on the wall?"

"It's the wireless modem," Kirk Milner, the evening Residential Counselor hastily responds.

Rita, wide-eyed, continues, "Since they have it there, how are they going to protect the patients from IT? I have heard of those wireless gadgets. The so-called modems can spy on and hurt us, especially me. Look at it. It has blue lights flashing all over it, and the blue lights go from side to side. It's just waiting to get at us."

Kirk tries to explain how the wireless modem works and why it is used.

"To Rita and all of you, the wireless modem is not something to hurt any of us. I wouldn't be here if it was going to hurt everybody in this room," he assures everyone. With the wireless modem, you can watch those 70's TV shows you all like. It also makes it possible for those of you who like to play games and research stuff on the Internet. That's how we get Internet in the building Rita."

Rita screams out, "I still want to know who's going to protect us from IT."

Kirk glances at Rita and at the other patients. He comprehends they are scared from their questionable expressions.

Now he says to himself, *how do I calm her down without upsetting the others? They do not have a clue what she is talking about and they have no idea she does not know.*

"It's out to get me," Rita continues. She will not let it go. When her voice sounds at such a high pitch, others in the room begin to fidget and await answers from Kirk.

Kirk gives it all he has. He reassures her, "Ms. Rita, it's not out to get you or anybody else."

He wants to calm her down first. She notoriously riles others; the room is heavy with unsettling movements and mumbles.

"Let me deal with the modem and the patients please," Kirk calmly and patiently tells Rita.

He knows he needs to stroke her just right.

Rita throws a medium-size book on the floor. She throws a second larger book at the modem and screams, "Don't hurt me, please."

Tom Holland, one of the ward assistants, comes in and gently escorts Rita out of the meeting and into the social worker's office. The recorded therapy session is over, cut short by Rita's frantic episode.

FAMILY AFFAIR

Mary accidentally shuts the player off. Her curly eyelashes flap to keep from falling asleep.

Malcolm walks in the room and sits on the couch.

Bobby plops on the recliner. "Whew I'm tired. Hi Mare, hi mom. What's going on with my two favorite ladies? Mom, when will we move again? I'm so ready to get out of this place, not just this house, but the neighborhood."

Malcolm turns around and glances at Mary, "Yeah me too."

Washing dishes, Ms. Sutton does a 180 with an expression of surprise. She asks, "Young men what's the reason for these questions? You know I have no plans of moving anytime soon."

Bobby and Malcolm eye ball each other and turn to their mom. Slyly they glance at Mary.

"Mary wants to move too." Malcolm eyes her insisting, "Ask her."

Mary is sitting, not saying a word, with a why are you bringing me into this conversation expression on her face. She's digging around in her purse as if she does not hear them or understand what they're talking about.

"Is this true?" Ms. Sutton asks.

"Mom, it's just the way the people treat me, the way they treat all of us in the family. Do you see it? I do not want to live in a place where the people do not like me. I have never done anything to them. There is no reason for them to treat us different from other people. We need to live in a neighborhood where we can feel welcome and comfortable; live in a place where neighbors want to help and not always put us down and make us feel unwanted.

Mary slowly gazes again in her purse, her voice rises, and cracks, and you hear a little sniffle. "We are a good family. There is never any trouble coming from our home. People do not hear us fighting or arguing. We love each other and we love GOD. Besides, we're nice to everyone."

"You know Sweetie you said it. We love GOD and GOD loves us. He will see us through. We have made it all these years. I know it is hard, but keep the faith. All we have is our love, faith, and hope. I love you all and will always be here for you."

Bobby is 13 years old and attends the local middle school. Appearances can be deceiving. At first glance, Bobby can give the impression of a hood type. His demeanor and smarts say otherwise. Make no mistake; he earns some of the best grades in his school. All grades are a high B average or above. He never gets in trouble. He takes himself and family seriously. If respect is what you want, respect is what you will get.

Malcolm is 10 years old and attends the local elementary school. An aspiring basketball player, he longs to play high school and college ball.

"Ya'll better get over here and help me rinse off these dishes," Ms. Sutton requests, her arms open ready to hold each of them. "I don't want to hear another word about moving.

Malcolm how was basketball practice today? When is your next game?"

"It's Saturday. Are you coming?"

"Are you playing home or away?"

"We are home this week and I want all three of you to be there. It'll make me so happy to look up while playing and see my three favorite people cheering for me."

Crossing his fingers Malcolm asks, "How about it Bobby and Mary? And you mom?"

"Well, when you put it like that, it's kinda hard for your ole mom to say no."

"I know right–count on your sis."

Out of the blue Ms. Sutton states, "Please be strong for me and your brothers. Most of all Mary stay strong for you. Keep your head held high."

∞

"I know what they say about me. I hear it sometime. I hear the whispers of me being a fruitcake or a nutcase. Why do people say things about me mom? I'm not a nutcase."

"I know Sweetie. People can be cruel, adults and children both. I am so sorry baby. I wish there is something I can do to make things better for you, for all of us. I try as hard as I can to keep things going and to keep the family together, with a roof over our heads and food on the table. No matter where a person lives, there will always be somebody to give them a hard time. That is the way life is. Try not to let it bother you. I know it's hard, but do not worry about other people. Most times, they have their own problems. People like getting into others personal and family matters. If they take care of their own affairs; they won't be in others business, including ours."

THREE YEARS LATER

Hello Mr. Bob and Mrs. Margareet, How are you doing today? I am on my merry way to bargain shop with mom. Is there anything you need?"

"We are good Mary, and we appreciate you thinking of us. Take care."

Some neighbor kids intentionally hang outside as Mary and her mom load in their car. They taunt Mary, and it spills over to Ms. Sutton. Mary unfortunately receives the worst of it. The expression of obvious pain is shown on both Mary and her mother's face.

Ms. Sutton supportively expresses to Mary, "I love you dear."

Tommy, a neighborhood teen, defends Mary and speaks up, "It's not okay to keep on disrespecting their family and picking on Mary. She is a sweet lady. Leave her alone. Go on, get out of here, and leave them alone. Have you ever heard of Karma? It's a bitch, so watch out."

Mary gets in the car with her mom; they whisk off down the back road.

"Look mom, I see a squirrel; watch out, there's a deer."

"Honey, I don't see anything. Where is it?"

Mary laughs, "Mom, this is going to be a good day. I love when we do things together. The boys are not here; it is just the two of us. It's so special."

"Thanks Baby, I love spending time with you too. It is so good when we can have our girl time. Spending time with all of you is special to my heart, but our girl time is at the top of my list."

Mary always has a smile on her lovely face and is friendly to everyone, even though she has a terrible loneliness that most others don't see.

"Mom," Mary screams in agony, "My head is banging all of a sudden. It hurts a lot."

"Did you take a migraine pill?" Ms. Sutton asks in a gentle voice.

"Not yet."

"What are you waiting on baby? Take something now so it can begin to work," Ms. Sutton suggests as she reaches to caress her hair.

Even those who do not know her well often refer to Mary as the nutcase with tits and a clit. Of course, most talk behind her back. She is a diagnosed schizophrenic, and to add, she experiences severe migraines. In the neighborhood, this awful illness carries a stigma. Hearing voices for at least ten years of her life, since the age of ten, is a long time for any person to suffer.

∞

Ms. Sutton pulls into the driveway. "Come on Mary; let me help you into the house first."

Malcolm asks, "Did you go shopping; do you need help with the bags?"

"You are a sweet son. Get the stuff in the trunk honey."

Mary goes straight to her room and closes the door. She anxiously scans around the room, up on the ceiling, and under the bed.

"What are you trying to say to me?" Mary yells out. "Why are you in my head? I don't want to hear from you today."

She hurriedly pops half of a white migraine pill and lies across the bed. Tossing and turning, woefully she says to herself, *I cannot get comfortable. What am I going to do? I can't ever get enough rest. The voices inside my head are mumbled, numbing, and not understandable. What are they saying? It sounds like a little baby talking all the time.*

Mary does not wait for or initiate trouble. Trouble seems to find her at every turn. In her eyes, the inflammatory remarks from others who do not know her are cruel.

BABY BROTHERS

Evening rolls around, and Bobby goes to his mom with a sensitive question. He fiddles with his hands for a minute. "Why don't girls show an interest in me?"

Viewing his mom and twisting his belt he says, "I'm a handsome dude. I know I am."

"You are so handsome. Soon you will be fighting off all the pretty young girls," Ms. Sutton reassures him.

He coughs and laughs, "I can't wait, and I hope it happens soon. I am always an extra wheel. I am trying not to complain too much because sometimes I am glad just to be a wheel. If it were not for being an extra wheel, I would not be doing anything with the other kids. The idea of being a fly on the wall and knowing what girls say and think about me is awesome. Are there any girls interested?"

Ms. Sutton joins in a laugh, "I know exactly what you mean. There are so many times I say how nice it would be to hear what people hide from you, like people from work, people who think they're better, and people who plot against you. The list can go on and on."

Mary has not made it yet. She usually is stirring about upstairs, but it's quiet.

Bobby knocks on her bedroom door; out of brotherly concern, he asks, "Are you sleeping? Are you working tomorrow? I don't know what it feels like but you can talk to me about how much it hurts. I love you."

He tries to understand when her unbearable headaches along with her other medical issues make it hard to cope and have a fruitful day.

"I just want to help you feel better Sis. What can I do for you?"

She tries to roll over and talk, but the pain will not let her. "Please just leave me alone. I need to rest. Jackhammers are attacking my head from all sides.

"Cut off the light."

"Okay."

Emotions of guilt and with pain in her voice, Mary says, "I'm sorry, thanks for caring; I love you."

Bobby goes to his darkened room. "I love my family. What can I do to help my sister? Help me Father; help me to be there for my sister, mother, and brother."

Lying there in his many thoughts, he jumps up and turns on the TV. He tosses, turns, and watches TV in bed. Three hours pass; glow in the dark numbers on the nightstand clock show 12:15 a.m. He needs to get to sleep; his mind wanders. He opens his journal ready to write what occurred for the day, but doesn't. He tries to sleep.

The continuous tossing and turning does not end. His life is complicated; His life is a family affair. He has his sister, his mom, and younger brother, his own life, and the neighborhood to deal with.

∞

With his mind racing and inability to fall asleep, he steps out of the house for a couple of hours.

I need someone to talk with me. I do not have a father to talk to when I have questions or feel so low down. Where is that understanding girl in my life? All I can do is try to keep it together, and try not to bother mom too much. She has enough to worry about with everything else including the other family issues and bills.

Bobby walks down the street and past the corner.

You know the corner.

"Hey Bobby, what's up man? Let me talk to you. I know your family is having hard times. Your mom is struggling and you have a sister with a mental issue, a younger brother to help support, and not to mention at your age, would you like to sport some better looking gear?"

With both hands held out, his head drops down to the right side; he skims over his clothes.

"Yeah Drayden, I would. I only make so much and almost all of it goes to helping my family."

"You would be surprised how many people realize you are a good person. That is cool, nothing's wrong with that. We need a lot of young men like that. You are a young man who makes your mom proud. With all that good talk about you, at the same time I can help you get the extra dough to buy those fly new clothes. I can help you out."

Bobby tries to play it cool. He naively asks, "What will I have to do?"

With a slight smile Drayden responds, "You will do something for me, things I will need."

"Do you sell drugs? My mother would not like it, she would not approve. I do not think so. I'll try to find extra money another way; thanks for thinking of me."

"Man you are turning down a good money making opportunity. Do not let it pass you up. Do you see how I dress and the cars I drive? Have you seen all the pretty women I have on my arm? You can have that when you're paid. Bobby you can be paid too, just like me."

∞

Bobby continues walking; he turns and heads for home. As he nears the house drops of rain hit his head, and he hears several loud rumbles of thunder.

The lights go out as Bobby walks through the back door. "Wow, something else to get on my nerves."

Mary calls out, "Bobby please check the breaker box."

Already on his way downstairs, the appearance of a whitish flash of light is startling. He quickly jumps back.

What was that?

A few seconds pass. The breaker switch flips; the entire house immediately lights up. He slowly turns the downstairs lights off, rushes toward the upstairs through the hallway, and up more stairs to his room. He happily climbs into his pillow-top bed, reaches for his personal journal, and writes.

As I look through my drawers for a decent pair of jeans and a shirt, I am a lot like any other young teenager; I want to be in style. Even through the pressure I feel of not being the stylish young man I see and know I can be, I try not to show it; I especially hide it from mom. She has enough problems of her own to deal with. I am not a free loader at home and I take care of my business. At only sixteen, I handle mine by trying to walk the straight and narrow. At sixteen, there are only so many legit jobs available to me.

When payday comes, I give about three fourths of the money toward helping with household and family bills. I do not mind and am not complaining. I am proud to be able to help mom. Most people do not understand what it is like when a family member has a disability. Whether it's a physical, emotional, or mental disability, usually more than just the person with the disability is affected. It affects others in the household. It often affects other family members outside of the household and friends.

This is where I am. I'm a cute, vanilla, 5'10", sixteen years old, trying to help hold it down.

The neighborhood, the few friends I have, school; none know what I have to deal with. I keep it all bottled up inside of me.

I don't want others to know. I want to seem normal to others. I want to start dating. There are several girls I am interested in, but I feel invisible to them. When I talk, they only talk to me as a friend, never as a possible boyfriend.

The pencil on the bed and journal on his stomach, he is slightly snoring.

Finally, Bobby is asleep.

∞

Bobby wakes, dresses, and oh so lightly slides out the back door. Where is he going at three o'clock in the morning?

"Drayden, I'm ready to try it."

"You are. What changed your mind? Never mind that. Here's a little something for you." He slides Bobby a couple of packets of heroin.

Within minutes, Bobby has a customer. They interact. He receives $20 and at the same time gives the man a packet. "This isn't that bad." With a smile on his face, he admits to Drayden, "I can see myself doing this." They exchange daps.

No sooner than the two give daps another customer comes down the street. "What do you want?" Bobby asks.

"What do you have?"

"$20 packets of heroin."

First Bobby slides the packet to the customer. He waits for the twenty dollars.

Oh no, the customer grabs Bobby. He says, "You are under arrest for selling drugs."

It is an undercover cop. He places Bobby in handcuffs.

"You have the right to remain silent. Anything you say can and will be used against you in a court of law. You have the right to an attorney. If you cannot afford an attorney, one will be provided for you."

Drayden walks away; Bobby eyeballs Drayden.

"No don't take me. This is the first time I have done this. I'm not really a drug dealer."

"Tell it to the judge."

"No, please. Please."

"Mama, Mama."

Bobby screams, "I need your help. Leave me alone." He writhes and jumps up, with a good view of himself and his surroundings.

It is only a dream!

THREE YEARS LATER

Mary get up; it's Thursday morning, and you have an appointment with your doctor. It is 6:45; please be ready by 8:15. Your appointment is at 9:00 a.m."

She turns, flops in the bed, and ultimately requests her mom's sympathy, "Mom I don't want to get up yet. I can hear the sound of jackhammers in my head. I need to lie here a little longer."

"No, I have let you stay in bed as long as possible. Come on get up."

Mary sits up in bed and moves her head from side to side. Finally, she rises to her feet and makes a quick stride to the bathroom. After washing her hands, she makes her way downstairs.

She pours milk from the refrigerator and discreetly places something in her mouth.

"Why aren't you taking a shower?" her mother asks as she notices the time from the clock on the wall.

"My head is hurting, so I'm taking my medicine now instead of waiting until after I eat."

She creeps back upstairs and lightly sits on the bed. *I'll lie back for a few minutes before I shower.*

Ten minutes later, "Mary, I don't hear the water running. What are you doing?" a flustered Ms. Sutton asks. "MARY."

"I fell back asleep. I'm getting up," she says in a not so eager voice.

She makes her way into the shower. The water glistens as it runs down her body.

"Bobby and Malcolm, both of you get up," another wake up request from mom.

"Malcolm, I'll drop you off at school and Bobby you can go into work thirty minutes early."

Bobby works three days of each week, Wednesday, Saturday, and Sunday late morning until evening. He has no vocational classes on Wednesday.

Mary is out of the shower and ready to dress. *I just do not feel good and do not want to decide what to wear today. I need some clothes; these same ole rags are getting on my nerves. It would be good to have a sister or friend in which to borrow clothes.*

Malcolm goes to the bathroom.

∞

Mary states, "I wish I had some new clothes mom."

Bobby overhears. He can tell she is not complaining; he also understands her truly expressing what she feels as a desperate need. He goes downstairs pacing with his head down, slowly taking a sip of juice. He paces a little more, and takes another sip.

Malcolm approaches, "Mom, I need some money for school. Do you have any?"

Her face shows some concern and she asks, "What is it for? I really don't have any money to spare."

"There's a sale at the school today, and I want to take five dollars to buy some things. If you don't have it to spare I can wait until next time."

"Love you mom, see you later," Malcolm lovingly professes, as he heads for the front door.

He is ready to leave with his jeans and striped shirt on.

As he walks out the door Bobby hurriedly yells, "Hey Malcolm, here's five dollar's for you big head. Enjoy!"

He runs and grabs the five dollars from Bobby. He checks out the green.

Surprise! It's a ten bill.

"Thanks Bro," with the big brother came through for me look on his face.

Mary and Malcolm head out the door at the same time.

She yells, "Bobby, Mom, come outside. Look at that rainbow in the sky. It's so beautiful."

"Did it rain last night?" Bobby asks. "It probably rained so hard a rainbow appeared."

DR. PERCY

Mary and her mom arrive at the doctor's office to a jammed parking lot.

"Go on up to Dr. Percy's office, wait for me. I will find somewhere to park.

"Make sure to sign in as soon as you get there, before you sit down."

Mary opens the door, where nine other people wait. She signs in and finds a spot with two empty chairs; she sits in one and places her handbag in the other, using it as a placeholder for Ms. Sutton.

Waiting for her mom, she flips through a beauty magazine.

Ms. Sutton walks in, and at the same time the office manager says, "Hello Mary, I see you have already signed in; Dr. Percy will see you shortly."

"Hi mom, we're waiting to be called. Look at all the people waiting."

"Hi, my name is Mary, what's your name?" introducing herself to a woman sitting there with a man. "I'm here because my head hurts all the time and I have another problem, but I won't talk about that. Why are you here?"

Before the woman answers, the medical assistant opens the door and calls, "Mary Sutton." She walks back, sits in the room, and patiently waits for Dr. Percy. Her mom soon follows behind. The doctor always allows her to attend during visits to know what is going on and keep up with Mary's progress. What better way than regularly sitting in on the doctor visit.

Fifteen minutes have gone by and Mary asks, "Mom what's taking so long?"

"Did you see all the people in the waiting area? I am sure many of the people are here to see Dr. Percy. He has other appointments before yours and after yours. They're just now letting previous people out and calling the people with the appointments scheduled around the same time as yours."

Approximately ten additional minutes of waiting, Dr. Percy walks in and closes the door. He briefly looks over Mary's chart and says, "Ms. Sutton, good to see you. Hi Mary, how are you doing today?

What has been going on with you lately? Did you start the goal list set last time you were here? I've been waiting to hear how it's been coming along."

"Doctor Percy," she responds with sadness. "I'm feeling depressed today. Actually, I have felt lonely and depressed for many days now, and it's getting worse. I still have bad headaches and they are worse when I'm depressed. My regular doctor, Dr. Vogo says I have migraines and other types of headaches. I have a headache all the time."

Recognizing her discomfort, he asks, "How are you coping with having headaches all the time and how does it make you feel?"

"I don't know what to do. I can't get rid of the pain. I ask GOD for his help all the time."

Mary has no control of her own existence when she is depressed and unhappy. She definitely understands, but the problem is she has nobody to share what she is going through. She can only talk to GOD.

I feel so alone. Who will understand? I hear voices and have crazy headaches. Nobody on Earth truly understands.

Dr. Percy turns and addresses Ms. Sutton. He asks, "Since you are with her every day how do you feel her treatments are progressing? Is she experiencing any gains?"

"Yes, there is some progress, but only a little. She still has those terrible headaches and the voices in her head. I hope the voice inside goes away. I am happy she will get to see her friends tomorrow. It is good for her to have friends and others to talk to away from home. It's good for her to be around other people she trusts," Ms. Sutton, sympathetic and loving mother expresses.

"We will continue to pray and thank GOD, for the friends he sent to her.

"It has been hard for us to bring a family member to see a psychiatrist. Historically our family has never done that. I love my daughter and she needs help. We know other families, people I work with and families of friends that use psychiatrist and mental health facilities regularly, some with good results and some with no changes at all. She has so many issues. I am not in her mind; I feel for her. She doesn't feel like there's any hope.

"My Mary is a regular down to earth girl. Being witty, scheming, and a do whatever it takes to make it; she just does not have that mentality. It is not that she is slow or has a mental learning disability. To Mary life should be easy; not this dog eat dog world that she is forced to be a part of, but does not understand or know how to deal with. There are people in this chaotic world who are innocent at heart. Mary is one of them.

"Dr. Percy, please explain why the treatment plans failed? The medicines are like trial and error and she is the guinea pig. It has been 16 years and I feel for her. Most of the time I wish I could take her place. I hate to see my child suffer. No matter how old she becomes she is still my baby and I will always worry about her. How long will she have to continue suffering? At first, the migraine medicine was helping some. Now it takes about three to five hours for the medication to take effect and help, if at all."

Mary jumps in, "Some of the pain goes away in about four hours, but sometimes it takes longer. The migraines never completely go away. If I do not have any migraine medication I cannot move; I cannot get up at all. The migraine never goes away; it just gets worse, covering my entire head."

Ms. Sutton assertively continues, "Doctor something has to be done. It is extremely bad and the migraines are excruciating. Her headaches have gone from two per month to once or twice per week."

"The voice inside my head is just as strong and talkative as ever before. When I leave work, my head hurts so bad I can barely walk or talk. Every time I want to be sociable, I am usually so tired and my head hurts so bad all I want to do is go home and crawl in bed. When I get home and lie down, I continue hearing vibrations and voices in my head. I hear voices all night and have headaches most of the day.

"My family is supportive but I want and need a friend, a friend of the opposite sex. The problem is nobody understands and usually does not care.

"Is there anything else you can do to help me? I know you are my psychiatrist, and I should open up about everything, but I really don't feel comfortable talking about everything going on with me."

Doctor Percy writes her new prescriptions for depression, anxiety, schizophrenia, and migraines. He says, "Make a follow-up appointment for two months from now."

"Is there anything else that can be done? Prescriptions do not help much; I've had these issues far too long."

She loudly screams, "Somebody please help me. I can't take it anymore. Nobody is taking tests. Dr. Percy, please!" She places her hands over her face; she balls and cries.

Ms. Sutton is gently giving her a reassuring hug. "It's okay honey, Dr. Percy is positive this prescription will help you, so let's go."

"Mom, take me to fill the prescriptions. I want to take them right away and go to bed."

Ms. Sutton wants to get Mary the best possible care, but without health insurance, the only option is to take her to the local mental health facility. Many people go; the facility fortunately accepts both State Medicaid and Social Security Disability Medicare coverage.

The local behavioral health facility doctor's diagnosis is Schizophrenia and Bipolar. A larger number of low-income persons and other individuals receiving government benefits go to this facility. It is always busy, a revolving door.

Mary continues to take the same medications; none of the others seems to work. Some family members have given up hope, but not her mother. Do not get it wrong; Ms. Sutton is weary. While extremely stressed she has unfortunately exhausted all resources. When Mary hears the voices, the migraines appear. Ms. Sutton refuses to give up hope. She tirelessly continues to pray for intervention and a miracle. Her undying faith will not let her give up.

∞

After returning home from picking up Mary's prescriptions, Ms. Sutton happily relishes in the idea of simply relaxing in her own room.

A MOTHER'S LOVE

Lord, please hear my prayer. I come to you this day as I have come to you every day. Please do not leave me. Bless my family. Place your love around us and touch my daughter. She has been suffering for so long. She loves you as much as I do. What are we to do father? Please don't forget our love. Guide us forever and give us almighty strength to keep enduring.

Mary falls on the floor holding her head, "My head is hurting right now." She cries out, "Mom I need help. My head is hurting and I hear scrambled voices."

RAIMEE

Mary's friend Raimee Alexander suffers from severe migraines and cluster headaches. For fifteen years, headaches inconveniently attack every day. Working in a professional office career her brain is critical in the functioning of daily job duties.

Ms. Sutton walks in the door.

"Mom, will you come to my basketball game? It's next Saturday at the school. I would like you to watch me play. All of you should come?"

"Where are Mary and Bobby?"

"Mary is lying down and Bobby isn't home yet."

"What time is your game next Saturday and how much does it cost to get in the gate? I will try to make it but you know it will depend on if I am up to it. Remind me on Thursday. Going to bed early enough Friday night will help me get up on Saturday. What time is kick-off?"

"I have to be there at noon. The game starts at 1:00."

"Like I said, I'll try to make it since I don't have to get up until 11:00."

Mary gets her phone and voice dials, "Call Raimee."

"Hello Mary."

"Are you still driving to the meeting?"

Raimee responds, "Yes, and I'll pick you up. I know you went to the doctor several days ago; what did he say? Did he make any changes to your treatment?"

Mary, two thumbs down, replies, "I broke down at Dr. Percy's office and asked them to take some tests. He gave me refills on migraine meds. I asked him for something else to help because the migraine and pain medicine do not work well. He didn't give me anything different. My emotions were out of control; I cried. The doctors just don't understand when you hurt all the time and nothing helps.

"What can we do?"

Raimee's face shows much discomfort. She responds, "Nothing, nobody understands. I know that in my case they look at me as if I am exaggerating about the severity of the pain. I can see it in their appearance and reactions. They wonder how I function and how I have worked all these years if I am bad as I claim. What they do not know is I am tired. I cannot take it any longer. The pain is debilitating. I cry all the time.

"Am I losing it? I am not sure. All I know is I want to feel better."

"I understand Raimee," is Mary's believable response. "It's the same with me. I have so much pain with no relief. It makes life unhappy, almost unbearable."

∞

Raimee, a complicated person, is a little older than Mary and keeps to herself most of the time. She totally presents a different personality.

Mary is outgoing, friendly, and trusting of everyone. Raimee emphatically understands; Mary does not have the life experiences she has. She still believes in and trusts most people. Her mind is at the point where no matter what people do to her or how they treat her she continues to trust.

Raimee cannot trust so easily; she encounters numerous backstabbers in her life. To many, Raimee is not as outgoing as they prefer. It is not the lack of trusting others that creates the introverted personality. There are other variables. Most do not understand what she is going through. She lives a complicated life. Too often, she knows what it is like to be in constant pain, never having the freedom to think, love, and have understanding. She has never-ending work, stress, and sickness, including people constantly trying to hurt and bring her down.

Due to Raimee being an introvert and not trusting of the outside world, her views about others is often perceived as imagining everyone is out to get her, although, in her situation she truly has problems.

Raimee sadly says, "There's one thing that will make my life happier." But with pain on her face she continues, "I'm not able to find that either."

MARY LOSES IT

I t's time to go to the grocery store," Ms. Sutton reminds Mary. She climbs into the car's driver side, and Mary jumps on the passenger side. Ms. Sutton drives about twenty-five miles per hour through the main neighborhood street.

Mary quickly rolls down her window, "Hi, Hi," she screams to all the people she lays eyes on.

It's a ten minute drive to the grocery store, so she has time for several greetings.

They pull into the parking lot, and they are ready to enter. The automatic door opens, and she hears a voice say, "Hi Mary, I didn't know you shopped at Grocer's Hub."

"I didn't know you shopped here Raimee."

"I come at least twice a week. This is my favorite store. Is that your mom who walked inside ahead of you?"

"Yes."

She follows her mom inside. "I'll call you tomorrow Raimee."

"Who is that," Ms. Sutton asks?

"Her name is Raimee," she gleefully responds. "She is one of my best friends."

She grabs the large buggy for her mom and another buggy for herself. "Mom did you bring the list of what we need?"

"Why haven't you talked about her or mentioned her name? She dresses nicely. What does she do?" Ms. Sutton tries to get an answer.

"Did you bring the list I asked of you before?"

"Yes, I did," pulling the scribbled list Mary wrote from her purse.

Mary goes down a different aisle than her mom. She places many different food types in the buggy. She tries to strike a conversation with some of the people at the store, and all she gets from them are smiles. A few speak and several do not. Others just look at her with a long stare and continue walking. "Let's get chicken, potatoes, ketchup and everything." While skipping the buggy down the aisle, she is acting six not twenty-six years old.

Mary can be a handful for Ms. Sutton. She puts on a show for everybody. She swings her hair back and forth, dances, sings, twerks, and does all the things she should not do in the grocery store.

"What is the reason for acting like this today?" Ms. Sutton calls to her, "Will you please come over here? Mary, please come here. I need you."

She is ignoring me. "Didn't I say come here?" Ms. Sutton sternly asks.

"I don't want to take them mom." Child-like Mary asks, "Do I have to? I feel okay."

Harboring a sneaky smile, she asks one of the customers in the store, "I'm not acting terrible, am I?"

"Come on Mary," Ms. Sutton asks, as she urges and begs. "I really need you to take your medicine."

She experiences agitation because of Mary's age. She wishes the doctor could find a course of treatment that keeps her on a steady path of healing mentally and emotionally.

Raimee is walking toward Mary viewing and hearing how she is acting with her mom. "Mary, girlfriend, you know we need to take our meds. Take what your mom is giving you. I have to take mine even when I do not want to, so you must do the same. If you don't listen to your mom I'm not coming to take you gallivanting around this weekend."

"What is gallivanting?"

"It's a word I say when I'm just riding around all over town with nothing really pressing to do and no place important I have to be, just for the fun of it."

Mary's attitude abruptly changes, "Okay mom, here I come, give me the pills."

Ms. Sutton goes into her purse, pours two pills in Mary's hand, and gives her a half bottle of water. "Thanks Ms. Raimee, I appreciate your help. I forgot to give her medication to control her actions before leaving for the grocery store. It usually takes about thirty minutes for the pills to take effect."

"Do not worry about it. No need to think twice; it's my pleasure to help."

Mary and Ms. Sutton continue to shop.

"My love for her makes me wish she can be Mary on the pills all the time. She acts her age when she is."

∞

Ms. Sutton, emotionally upset calls Bobby on the phone. "My daughter, your sister, listens to strangers instead of me. She would not take her meds for me at the store but did for a friend of hers. I am thankful for the friend–just not sure I want her listening to others instead of me. Mary should listen to me. I'm her mother."

"Mom, do not let it bother you. You know Mary acts totally different when she takes her pills regularly."

Ms. Sutton hesitates and remarks, "Alright, see you at the house in about fifteen minutes."

MEETING ONE - GROUP

A family calendar hangs on the wall. It helps Mary, Malcolm, Bobby, and Ms. Sutton keep up with all their important reminders, appointments, and events. Mary views the calendar for her next doctor's visit and her other meetings. Her next important event listed is attendance at her outpatient meeting.

"I'm going to my meeting tomorrow," Mary says to her mom as she looks at the calendar.

A two-year in-patient of the San Lumen's Hospital, a behavioral health facility, Mary released to out-patient status now attends weekly meetings and continues her psychiatrist visits. Ten other patients regularly attend the meetings on her scheduled days. All in-patient releases must regularly attend the out-patient meetings. The weekly meetings help the client and the doctor manage.

"I don't want to go," Mary would share all the time before entering the in-patient program.

She asserts, "I now prefer out-patient. Out-patient meetings allow me to visit the friends I made while an in-patient. I'm older and friends are so important to me.

"Donnie Williams, Lara Walton, Tia Ramsey, and Richard Clemson are other patients I've built personal relationships with at the centers. I met Donnie and Tia while a resident at the in-patient care center, Lara, and Richard since attending weekly out-patient meetings. It's the only time I have people to talk to other than my family and at work. Lara and Richard have been attending out-patient for eight years and the meetings are the only time I get to catch up."

∞

Mr. Nick Boggs is the out-patient counselor. The meeting gets underway. Everybody gives a quick hello and his or her names.

Mr. Boggs stands to ask, "Jody Summers, please reflect on your past week."

Jody kicks off the discussion by making everyone aware his mother died. Everyone knows this because it's been four months since her passing; he shares at every meeting.

Next, he asks Lara, "Will you discuss what happened last week in your life?"

Lara, with her head down answers, "Not tonight, Please!"

Mr. Boggs shakes his head with understanding and moves on to the next person. "Now Mary, it's your turn to share your past week with us. Would you like to share tonight?"

Mary hesitates briefly; she does not want everybody to know the full spectrum of what she deals with.

She opens by stating, "I'm so lonely, I hear a voice inside, and I feel unloved. That is it in a nutshell. I told my doctor that not many people, male or female are interested in hanging with me or being my friend. I don't even have a boyfriend."

"Will you also share your coping mechanism with us?" Mr. Boggs continues to ask.

Mary does not respond.

Raimee loudly sniffles and wipes her eyes.

Mr. Boggs waits until Mary finishes before asking, "Raimee how are you feeling? Would you like to share with the group tonight?"

Raimee's slightly lowered voice answers, "Mr. Boggs can I talk to you separately? I'll share with the group some other time."

Mr. Boggs calls for a fifteen-minute break.

Sasha Tiegs slides over to Mary and strikes up a conversation, "Mary, I've noticed from your discussions you are interested in animals, community, and helping people. I am interested in some of the same things. We have a lot in common. Would you want to be in a mentor relationship? I will support you when you need it. We can even do things together if you would like. Let me know what you think."

Raimee discusses with Mr. Boggs at the meeting, "I feel for Mary because she is a seemingly genuine person. I wish the best for her. Since she is not a troublemaker I wish her happiness. She wants to feel normal."

Mr. Boggs begs the question, "What is normal? In actuality, who is really normal?"

"What is normal? To tell the truth I'm depressed, anxious, and out of sorts a lot of the time; maybe I fit in the same category with Mary.

"I'm serious," Raimee proclaims. "I'm not sure if there are any truly normal people. Mary in most ways is normal to me. If people in the neighborhood weren't already aware Mary had issues she could possibly get by with not being talked about."

"People are cruel."

Raimee remarks, "Mary, I feel you, I feel the same way. Everything is so overwhelming. I am so alone all the time, I feel nobody loves me and there is nobody for me. I am lonely for companionship; I need to have a boyfriend to love me, to truly love me, and make me feel special.

"I have the weight of Atlas on my shoulders and there has never been a better half for me to share that weight with. Everybody mistreats me. Earth feels like a trapped location to suffer at the hands of everybody and nobody became trapped here for me. My heart is heavy, ripped out all the time. I don't know what I have to do to make people see me for who I am and show me love.

"When I say this, I'm not just talking about a man. It will be nice to have good work relationships, friends, and basically a feeling of respect from others.

"I have gone from a healthy twenty two year old to a thirty something and suffering. I always suffer in silence. I started a new job that paid decent money and within two weeks of being on the job, I began experiencing severe migraines. It was a new job and I was on six months probation; therefore, taking time off scared me.

"So day after day co-workers saw this false face within a body wracked with pain and frustration, putting it mildly.

Raimee sobs profusely; uncontrollable tears stream down her face. "Where is my love, my loyalty, and my friend? Where is my partner? I have no earthly love. If it were not for the Father above, I would not experience unconditional love at all. I have nobody to talk to about all the misconduct imposed on me by those I must deal with on a regular basis."

There is no denying the energized anxious feeling in the air. Gestures, tears, sniffles, and the sucking up of whimpers fill hearts with undeniable sympathy and empathy.

After the meeting, a woman with a smile and hello approaches Raimee. "How are you doing tonight? My name is Lakeeda Jamison. Your story and courage touches my heart. I work as an Executive at IVM Solutions. Will you allow me to be your support mentor? We might have a lot in common, and it would be nice to have someone to talk to." Lakeeda glances at Raimee with a questionable expression on her face. "What do you think?"

Raimee places her hand to her head without giving Lakeeda a response.

"What's wrong?" Lakeeda asks.

Raimee's eyes squint in pain, and she answers, "My head hurts."
She experiences heavy vibrations pulsing through her head. Voices run through her head at the same time, but she does not share the full details with Lakeeda. Raimee frantically tries to get away from Lakeeda; she wants to go home.

Lakeeda asks, "Can I get your number?"

"Okay, my number is 300-304-0001; I have to go. Call me tomorrow, goodnight."

"Goodnight," Lakeeda responds, as Raimee runs out the door and takes off in her car.
The car swerves doing about 65 mph in a 40 mph speed zone. Does Raimee understand how fast the speedometer registers? Does she even care?

∞

Raimee pulls up to the house, swings in the driveway with a hook, and jumps out of the car; quick as a jackrabbit she steps to the porch.

Although the lights shine brightly, her house door key misses its way into the key lock hole. Trying the door a second time, the keys fall on the porch. Grabbing her head, and at the same time saying, "Please help me, I need to get in and lie down. Please GOD, help me."

She takes her shoes off as she makes it to the bedroom; it takes all she has to muster the strength to crawl into bed. She falls on top of the cover and stretches out as if dead–no movement, nothing for several minutes. Her arm flails, her head moves from side to side, and the room fills with effortless sounds of moans and groans fill the room. Barely lifting her head, she reaches for a tiny white pill, the size of a match head and pops it into her mouth.

"Oh GOD, my head still hurts." She manages to lift her head to view the clock. Its two hours later, she drops another tiny white pill in her mouth and slowly drifts off to sleep.

TWO-FACED

At work, Raimee is sitting in Tareice Washington's office. Tareice is gossiping to Raimee one of many times about their co-workers.

"Richard is so stupid. He needs to get himself together.

"I am glad you did something with Veronica's hair. I don't know what is on her head. Somebody needs to work on it all the time. And thank you for fixing her wig. Girl that thing is cock-eyed one day and crooked the next.

"What about your boss' hair? It looks like a pile of poop sitting up on top of her head. What did she do—with that big crazy looking part in her hair?

"Girl, I cannot stand Lecretia as a boss. She does not know what she is doing. Nobody really likes her as their boss. She thinks she knows everything and sends everything in writing.

"Our second boss in line does not do anything. He is worthless. Show me what he does and I will show you driving the work vehicle like a family car. Even the family considers it their car. I heard one of his kid's say this is my daddy's car.

"She drives the work vehicle for her own personal use all the time but when I ask to use it for the weekend she won't allow it.

"Girl, Quinton needs to put some lotion or something on his hands and legs. He is so ashy all the time. I guess that is how he gets his women. That ash must have special fingers.

"Let me tell you about Tyson. He asks me on a date a while back and girl he wanted me to pay. After we had eaten, he walked outside of the restaurant and left me in there to pay the bill. All the other women I have talked to say he did the same thing to them. And don't let me get started on his stuff. Girl he does not have anything.

"Mr. Big stuff, ha ha ha!!

"Have you really looked at Kellum? The next time he is around take a good one; he looks like Mr. Potato Head. Good thing he is with Vera; who else wants a Mr. Potato Head.

"Girl don't he look like Mr. Potato Head?"

∞

"Now don't repeat anything I say."

"I won't," Raimee immediately replies. She simply goes with the flow.

Tareice continues, "Girl, Nanette is a trip. She let that fat guy take her for almost all of her income tax return and he left her and moved away. I don't know what her new man sees in her. She is dumb as a box of rocks. I asked my husband if he thought she was cute because she has a big butt, and he said she might have a big butt, but she also has an ugly mug."

She always has me rolling; I usually laugh so hard tears run down my face. I look at her wondering why she is talking about everybody. I know she is trouble because she has talked about every person on the job. Everybody is her friend; they absolutely love her, and have no idea she talks about each of them like a dog. I have figured her out. Although, I began to realize Tareice was somebody I needed to watch out for; she is one who actually scares me. She is a two-faced, conniving heffer.

She also claims Nanette is one of her closest friends.

FAMILY TIME

Going back to the neighborhood, Ms. Jansen, the trouble making, nosy neighbor across the street always talks about Mary to other people. The community likes Ms. Jansen because of her wealth of knowledge about everybody else's business. She makes sure to give the latest and greatest scoop on or about practically everyone. She talks trash and makes sure the neighborhood knows of Mary's problems. Most people in the community already know of Mary. Ms. Jansen's help is never necessary as the role she plays to make sure everybody gets the low down, dirty, incorrect dirt.

Mary walks in the house after her day at work; the family sits in the living room in front of the TV. She asks, "What's on tonight?"

"Well hello Sis, what's up with you? Did you eat yet? Mom cooked and your food is waiting for you. Look in the microwave; it's probably still warm."

Mary removes her plate of dinner from the microwave. "I'm starving, and this looks good." Commencing to eat while walking to the table, she asserts, "It tastes as good as it looks."

"Take your time," Malcolm remarks, smiling. "You're eating so fast; do you even know what it is?"

Mary laughs, "I know. It tastes so good. You know mama's cooking is the best." She is smiling, slightly laughing, and licking her fingers.

"I'm glad you enjoyed it sweetie."

"Thanks mom, you know what I'm going to do now."

"I know."

"Pass out sleep," Malcolm remarks, as he giggles.

"I sure am, but stay up for a while to watch a movie with ya'll."

Ms. Sutton, a loving mother, works hard to continue taking care of her children of three. "I sit here thinking about what will happen to the three of you if something happens to me. Please stay together. You need to be there and always take care of one another. Never let any other person come between you. If something happens to me, take care of each other. It is important to learn now, even if you meet a person and fall in love, to never forget about or quit looking out for one another. Please, please listen to me. Please promise me.

Ms. Sutton flips through the movies on the shelf and slides one gently into the player. "Turn off the lights, its family time," she exclaims, as she rushes to her seat with a happy to be with my family smile."

"It's the bank heist movie," Malcolm responds with excitement!

The family enjoys quiet times watching movies together; it means a lot to them. Family time turns out as a great time for bonding even if the Sutton family does not envision the blessing. Mary curls up on the couch, tilting her head back and to the side. Malcolm grabs a seat after pouring three bags of microwave popcorn into a huge bowl for everybody to share. After about ten minutes, Mary angles her body to make herself a little more comfortable.

With excitement and anticipation, Ms Sutton says, "Get ready, the movie is about to start and I love this movie! We watch it all the time; each of us should know every scene and word by heart," she snickers.

They all laugh and agree.

"Wait I forgot the drinks," Malcolm adds. He quickly jumps up and heads for the kitchen. "I'm gonna grab a two liter and some cups."

Ms. Sutton pushes the pause button.

"Mom let the movie continue."

Malcolm sits on the couch in time for opening credits.

Mary snores before the opening credits finish.

Malcolm reaches out to poke her forehead for a reaction, but before he can,

Ms. Sutton states quickly while whispering, "Leave her alone; let her sleep."

Thirty minutes later within a quiet room, Mary lifts her head and voices, "I'm going to bed, see ya"ll in the morning." She walks to the bedroom as if sleepwalking and crawls into bed. She never misses a beat and immediately falls asleep.

Twenty minutes later Malcolm stands and says, "Mom I hear talking. It's coming from Mary's room."

They do not pay much attention. Mary is schizophrenic; they are used to hearing her talk to herself.

This talking sounds different.

With a puzzling look on his face, Bobby questions, "Is she talking in her sleep?"

Mary screams out.
They run into the room to find her asleep.
Everybody exits the room and closes the door.

"We might as well go to bed too," Bobby says.

Goodnights said.

"Love both of you," mom declares.

About twenty minutes later, Ms. Sutton goes back to check on Mary. She cuts the light on, looks at her and looks around the room, as if something does not appear right. She flips the light switch to off, returns to her bedroom, turns on the dimmer light, and opens her usual book to read.

Mary twists and turns most of the night. She wakes up with unexplainable night sweats. Her clothes, sheets, and cover are all soaking in sweat. Determined to get back to sleep she changes the sheets and sleeping clothes. She does fall to sleep, only to wake, and sit straight up in bed full of sweat. Again, she changes clothes and throws a dry blanket across the wet sheets. She cuts the fan on in hopes it reduces the night sweats.

∞

Mary wakes up at 7:00 a.m. to get ready for work. Everything is soaking wet, and with the fan blowing, her body feels frozen. Her schedule time to be at the store is 8:30 a.m.

∞

It is 8:00 a.m. and Mary heads to work arriving at the store to punch in at 8:20 a.m. After punching the clock, she immediately begins stocking some of the store items the last night shift did not finish.

Russ, the other associate, arrives at 9:00 a.m. "Why are you stocking this early Mary?"

"For the same reason you always walk in and see me stocking."

"It wasn't finished last night?"

"You got it."

∞

He exhibits a puzzled look on his face, and says, "Girl, you scared me, you screamed out."

One hour later, Russ slowly approaches Mary.

"Oh my goodness Russ, I had a dream last night. I'm just now remembering it."

About fifteen minutes later, Mary continues, "Oh man, I remember several dreams with many different things going on."

PROFESSIONAL RAIMEE

Raimee is one of the smartest people I know," Mary exclaims. "She has a degree in Accountancy and Business Management. Although, not schizophrenic she has many bodily ailments. She hurts constantly and has for thirteen years. Her diagnosis is cluster headaches, tension headaches, and migraines. That is four types of pain all in one head at the same time. I feel sorry for her. She has a professional job and her brain is important in the work her daily job duties require."

"Lakeeda, others give me uneasy looks; always responding to me as if I'm an idiot and as if they are the smartest. I do not like to feel incompetent and I do not like to feel that people are looking down at me all the time. I know I have above average smarts, so why do others rarely give me a chance to finish talking? Why do others try to make me believe I don't fit into their world?"

"Raimee are you being paranoid?"

"No Mary, I am not. You should hear some of the things that people say. The worst part of it is a lot of negative and judgmental comments come from the mouths of people who are not expected to judge, abuse, and manipulate others, supposed religious goers."

"Why don't people understand how they treat others?"

"Mary, the world is a weird place; some of the best people have it the worst. Unfortunately some people truly enjoy treating others terrible."

"Why?" Mary naively asks.

"Simply, it's the society we live in. When I say some people receive joy from others pain, they truly do."

"Nobody really knows what I deal with on a day-to-day basis. The work I do every day, dealing with people external and internal to manage my job, paperwork, and numbers all day. So using my brain is crucial. The facade on my face is good for work each day. Even after employment at the same company for over a decade, they really do not know. They tend to believe they know me. They see me reserved, private, devoted, but lacking certain skills because of being private and reserved. Yet they do not really see me. They do not have a clue.

"I see me, a person with so much to offer so many. In my professional and personal life, my work ethic is just that; I have a very good work ethic. This does not work well in a culture where everybody is into everybody's business. I have loosened up a little over the years, selectively giving the little information I want them to have.

"Nevertheless, no matter what I do and no matter how hard I work, my co-workers constantly throw me under the bus. I am reserved because of the sorry way I am treated. How is it that everybody can treat me like crap? Is there a sign on me that says it is okay to treat me like shit? Take a real good look.

"One reason people don't relate very well to me is because I don't do a lot of the normal things that most people do like gossip, scheme, and throw people under the bus.

"On any given day, boring as it might sound, I love watching the history, learning, rehab, cooking, and documentary channels. I love to learn constantly; what I love even more is watching how different people act. It is natural for me.

"I do not have a degree in Psychology or Social Work. What I have learned comes from experience and a great understanding that does not require receiving higher degrees written on a piece of paper from textbook studies. I have a Bachelor of Science and am mostly self-taught, reading as much, and experiencing more than most people with Graduate and Doctoral degrees.

"I am weird," Raimee exclaims about herself. "From experiences I have a Doctorate in Philosophy, Sociology, and Psychology."

"Don't say that about yourself. You are not weird; you are beautiful and special," Lakeeda says with kind reassurance.

∞

Mary questions, "Why don't you learn how to kiss a little bit of butt on your job?"

Standing up for her, Raimee responds, "I'm not a butt kisser. I should be; I wish I could be. I have always done my work while the butt kissers always get the kudos. I am nice to everyone and I converse with everyone. I just don't start trouble or act two-faced."

"Well you need to learn to be a butt kisser especially now that the culture is changing. It changed a couple of times and see what happened to you. Can you imagine what's in store for you now? Watch your back Raimee. I'm simply repeating what you say to me."

"I do not have time to watch my back like many other people. I am too busy doing all the grunt work. And it is awful funny I am not only the manager for several programs, I have to perform most of the work to ensure the quality.

"More than twenty years ago I thought differently from most people. It has always been like this. Even as a teenager, I did not succumb to peer-pressure. I was the odd ball, the odd girl out. Is this why I cannot relate to most people? I am still the odd ball. Now I am the odd woman out.

"When talking to people it is as if they look through me. They even talk over me. It is hard to and I cannot explain how I feel.

"Ever since I was a little girl I felt like I did not belong, and that nobody, not one person understood me. As a young girl I felt like an alien, always praying to GOD–trying to find a way to understand ME."

MARY'S NIGHT

Mary walks down five blocks and turns right. She crosses the street and goes inside Community Mart where she works. As she enters, the store clerk remarks, "Mary, you have a message from Raimee to call her ASAP."

She voice dials before punching the clock. "Hi Raimee, did you call?"

"Hello Mary, how are you? What are you doing after work next week and the weekend?"

"Nothing."

"The usual."

"Spending time with my family."

What her co-workers do not know is she will see friends at her weekly out-patient meetings. Mary looks forward to these meetings.

She expresses, "I want to be included in simple living and have a regular life. If my life is an open book, I tell what I go through, the meetings I attend and the people I see, it would be gossip central. I have been dealing with this for as long as I can remember. I am now an adult and treated like a crazy since a child. As an adult, I understand my issues. I also understand wanting and needing love, true love and understanding.

"I have had a hard time dealing with daily migraines and life's daily existence like most people. My problems are keeping me down physically, mentally, emotionally, and socially. With that said, I want pretty much the same things as other persons; but due to physical, mental, and emotional issues a serious hurt has been placed on my social life. At 26, life gets very boring. I do the same thing all the time and never have a chance to do things with others. I only have people to share with who have disabilities like mine. Although, believe me, I enjoy each of the friendships I make due to my disability."

Later in the evening, at home, there is a knock, knock at the door.

Malcolm hesitantly asks, "Who is it?" as he slowly and lightly walks to look through the peephole. "Who is it? Mary there is a guy at the door for you. He says his name is Donald Maddox."

Mary walks over and opens the door. She blushes and greets, "Hi Donald. Come in, have a seat. I'm glad you decided to come over.

This is my family; my mom, Ms. Sutton; Malcolm and Bobby, my brothers."

"We're getting ready to eat; join us for dinner," Ms. Sutton requests.

"Sure, I would love to eat with you all. Not that it matters but what's for dinner?"

Malcolm responds with a crooked smile on his face, "I thought it didn't matter."

Just in time Ms. Sutton chimes in, "Donald we are having meatloaf, mashed potatoes, and corn."

Nobody talks during dinner, only eating and some awkwardness.

After dinner, without hesitation, Donald asks, "Mary would you like to go for a walk in the neighborhood?"

Malcolm jokingly says, "Mary's got a boyfriend; you go Mary. I'm just playing Sis; I hope you have fun with, what's his name?"

"Oh Malcolm leave your sister alone," she suggests, with a slight smile. Ms. Sutton does have her concerns; this is the first young man to show an interest in Mary in years. She gives the young man a request, "Donald take care of my daughter while you have her out. She's in your hands."

Confident Donald replies, "I will Ms. Sutton, you can trust me."

Bobby gazes with his eyes up in the air and says in a low voice, "You better."

Twenty minutes later, there is a big sigh of relief and a smile on Ms. Sutton's face when Mary walks through the door. "It makes me feel somewhat better that Mary has someone in her life right now to fill a void; someone is giving her some well needed attention."

"I had a good evening," Mary tells Donald. "See ya."

Mary is still working, but work is becoming increasingly hard for her. The people at her job do not understand what goes on with her. They only see what they want to see, only the outside shell. People continue to talk about her behind her back. She can feel the eyes and whispers as she walks pass. Some people are cruel.

"I want to quit working. Paying bills and living keeps me going every day," Mary exclaims with sadness in her eyes.

Her mother says, "Most people feel that way. I feel that way myself. I would not go to work and put up with the two-faced people I have worked with all my life if I did not have to. Life is hard baby. You have me, and as long as I am on this Earth, you have me on your side. I will always stand by you."

Mary goes to bed and falls asleep within fifteen minutes.

∞

Morning rolls around, its 6:00 a.m. and Mary is up. Her schedule is to open the store at 9:00 am, but she needs to be there by 7:30 to stock shelves.

Already at the store, she punches in at 7:15 am. At 8:45, she takes a ten-minute break. Returning at 8:55, she places the money drawer in the register in time to open the doors at 9:00 a.m.

∞

Darkness sets in; it is five o'clock and Mary's shift is over.

"Hello," Mary answers her phone.

Raimee responds quickly and without a return hello, "I can take you home, but I don't get off for another ten minutes. If you can wait on me I'll be happy to pick you up."

Raimee works a twenty-minute drive from Mary's work.

Mary is not closing the store for the night. There is plenty for her to do to keep busy while waiting on Raimee. She punches out at 5:02 p.m., walks outside and walks back in.

Raimee wants Mary to wait for her. As a reminder, 5:05 p.m. she rings her phone again. "Don't leave Mary. I do not want you walking late and in the dark by yourself. Find something to do at the store until I get there."

"Okay. Okay," Mary instantly agrees.

Five minutes later, at 5:10 when Raimee calls the store, Mary left to begin the five-block walk to her house.

Five-thirty Raimee pulls up at the store. She appears upset because Mary did not wait. Mary does not seem to get it; danger lurks for a woman who walks home alone in the dark.

∞

At home, Mary is lying on the bed; her head hurts.

Ms Sutton asks, "Is there anything I can do for you? You work over eight hours and make that long walk home. That could be the cause of your migraine.

She turns off all the lights, TV, and computer; she places an ice pack around Mary's neck.

After forty-five minutes Ms. Sutton goes back to check on Mary; she is sleeping. She goes to bed also.

∞

Sometime during the night, Mary dreams of a small weird figure looking down at her. The figure, not intimidating or expressing harm, is scanning her from top to bottom and communicating using weird sounds.

The dream briefly wakes her. She checks around the dark room, in her bed, and under her bed. Within minutes she falls back to sleep.

MEETING TWO - GROUP

Night turns into morning, the sun rises, and Mary's alarm clock rings.

Sleepily reaching to turn the alarm off, Mary says to herself in a groggy, scratchy voice, *Time to get ready for another day of work; gotta make that money.*

Luckily, her headache is partially gone and she feels better.

However, she cannot seem to get the dream of aliens out of her head. Even though she went straight to sleep again, the dream is very vivid, as real as if it actually happened.

She thinks aloud. *They were aliens, sort of like the ones seen on TV. It appears some people are right about the existence of aliens.*

Afterwards, Mary eases out the door and heads to work.

The phone rings as Mary walks to work. It is Ms. Sutton, "Mary, don't forget you have your out-patient meeting this evening. Do you need me to take you?"

"I'll let you know mom. I want my friend to take me, but I'm not sure if she will be able. I'll call you back when I get a break. Thanks, I love you."

∞

While at work, Mary calls her friend Raimee, "Are you driving to the meeting?"

"Yes, and I'll pick you up."

∞

Raimee speaks out during the meeting, "I changed from a healthy twenty-two year old to a sickly now thirty-three year old.

"I have always suffered in silence. The first month after graduating college, I began working at a large company with great pay and excellent benefits. During the first week of work, my boss gave me the task of writing a computer program for the entire department's use. To learn the program, the following Monday I started a special class on programming. If successful, the program would retrieve data lost in space that the IT department's software was unable to capture. Of course, this was a new venture for me. After the week of programming class, it took approximately two months to program the report, test it, and make it work properly.

"But within two weeks of the start of employment, I began experiencing severe headaches and unexplainable body pains every day. I went from perfectly healthy to head and severe body aches every day. I was very sick and should have missed work but was scared for it to happen. Rightfully so, I was on a six month probationary period. So day by day, I went to work using this false face within a body wracked in pain. Remarkably, the report worked with accuracy. It was able to pull all the information that their expensive software captured and left out there in space.

"During this two-month period, none of the people I worked with knew how sick and wracked with pain I had become, or that I had developed chronic health issues since the start of employment. They had no idea the pain my body felt, the headaches and suffering I endured daily, and how my head roared and vibrated all day, every day. I was a professional, not a complainer.

"I worked at this company for ten years with many backstabbers and a non-caring upper management boss who did not even know my name. He called me Pam as short for Raimee, instead of Raimee.

"Who the hell is Pam?

"Later I was hired to work at another job where I am currently still employed. My migraines are worse. I never tell the boss or co-workers of my headaches or ailments. I am afraid if my employer learns of my true suffering and ailments it will jeopardize my employment. I am always afraid to confide in my co-workers and boss, and this incident and employment affiliation is no different."

Raimee knows if this knowledge makes it to certain people it is enough for them to find a way to get her fired. So, she continues to keep her mouth closed.

"My employer doesn't appreciate me and will use anything as a weapon. I continually pray that the Lord delivers me from the bondage and grasp of all those who mistreat, disrespect, and form weapons against me. I want to be with those who have my best interest at heart. I faithfully wait for the LORD to place me where I should be.

"I am telling the group how I feel. Mary, do not discuss our conversations or what you hear in-group with anyone in your neighborhood, not even family. I trust you and I would not want bad things to get back to my boss. It could get me in trouble and possibly cause the loss of my job. I know how these people are. Do not post anything on social media either. Can I trust you to keep everything you hear to yourself?"

∞

Mary eyes Raimee with an unsettling glance as if to say, too late, I've already ran my mouth.

Raimee senses something amiss and requests, "Mary promise you didn't say anything. Did you?"

Mary swears no but still Raimee worries.

"I have to be cautious, I need my job. It will be hard to start over especially being older and sick. I don't want to have to look for another job."

"Why are you so worried about your job? I've never seen anyone as worried as you."

"It is because where I work the bosses and co-workers are all two-faced and have their favorites. It is not who works the hardest or is most dedicated. It is the one with the best bull game. Since I am a doer not a bull shitter, I am always on the losing end.

"One of the bosses accused me several times of being the reason why certain things are or are not happening for the organization. I have worked my ass off for this company with no thanks. Literally, I see people sit around and play on their phone all day with nothing said. I say over and over, GOD doesn't like ugly."

One of Mary's friends at group invites her for lunch and a later meeting at her house. Mary, the thoughtful person she is, asks, "Can I bring my friend Sasha? You will like her; she is a good person."

Her friend responds, "It is okay."

She answers her phone, "You've got Sasha, who is this?"

"Hi, it's Mary. My friend from group invited you and I to lunch and then to her house. Will you go with me?"

Sasha briefly pauses and says, "Let me cook for you Mary. If things are bad for you now it is the least I can do to help you. I felt this about you. We all need someone who cares and I want you to know I do care about you.

"But yeah, I'll go with you. Are you sure your friend will be okay with me coming?"

"Yes she is good with it."

FLASHBACK

Annette, my co-worker asked, "Why are you so secretive about your personal life?

"I cannot believe you want to get to know a man because you are so secretive. How can someone get close to you?"

I responded, "The reason I don't let any of you get close to me is because of how I'm treated at work. That is the reason I do not like doing personal things with any of you. Why would I? All of you treat me like shit. I do not want to work with most of you much less spend after work time with you. I am not in the clique, so I am always made to feel like an outsider."

FRIENDS

Mom, I asked Raimee and Sasha over for dinner. I truly like both of them; we are becoming close friends. They understand me.

"Sasha is my age and even though she is normal, we spend more time together and have so much fun. I don't know what it is mom," Mary confesses. Her words carry so much feeling. "Since I met Sasha things have been different. She is a true friend. Raimee is a true friend also."

"Do you trust them?" Staring in her eyes for confirmation, Ms. Sutton asks.

Smiling and shaking her head up and down, "Yes I do. Both of them treat me special."

"Okay, it should be okay. I want to meet everyone who interests you. Have both of them stop by this Friday evening for dinner if they can. I want to get to know the people you care about."

"Thanks mom, you're great."

"How old are they?" Bobby asks, with that young man vibe. "Are they cute?"

"You'll be able to find that out when both of them come over Friday, silly."

Thursday evening Raimee bakes a chicken casserole.

Sasha bakes a yellow cake. She plans to frost it with milk chocolate frosting.

∞

Friday evening the doorbell rings. Tinka barks and runs to the door; Baby stays on the couch purring.

Raimee hands Ms. Sutton a casserole dish. Sasha hands her a cake.

"Thank you. Thank you. I did not expect you to bring anything but I am glad you did. Please have a seat in the living room; we will eat shortly."

Mary gestures her readiness to make introductions, "Mom, Bobby, and Malcolm, I'd like you to meet my friends Raimee and Sasha."

Malcolm affectionately expresses, "Wow both you ladies are pretty."

"Down young man," Ms. Sutton relays.

∞

Everyone finished dinner over two hours ago. Raimee and Sasha are home tucked in their beds. The Sutton's have finished dish duty and retired to their rooms.

∞

The next day, Saturday, all Suttons complete household chores. Malcolm vacuums the carpet early so he can be on time for basketball practice. Mary washes dishes, Bobby takes the garbage out to the curb, and Ms. Sutton washes clothes.

Every other weekend either Mary visits Sasha or Sasha visits Mary. This week Mary visits Sasha.

Bobby, Malcolm, and Ms. Sutton are growing fond of Sasha.

∞

Three weeks later Raimee invites Mary, Lakeeda, and Sasha to dinner. She meets them at the Asian Grill. Each week Mary has a chance to see Raimee and Sasha at the out-patient group meetings.

∞

Three months pass; Sasha and Mary continue growing closer.

"Mary, you are such a sweet person; I really enjoy being around you. Do you want to go to the mall this Saturday? I will pick you up around 3:00 p.m."

"Of course I do; Although, I don't have money for shopping."

"Girlfriend, do not worry. I have you. Be ready at three."

One tear rolls partially down the right side of Mary's cheek. "Which mall do we visit?"

"Prater Garden Mall; Prater Garden is the happening mall. There are lots of shops and a good food court. Wear something you can take off fairly easy in case you find some outfits you want to try on."

∞

On Saturday Sasha and Mary arrive at the jam-packed mall.

"So many cars, I hope we find a spot."

"I come to the mall all the time when it's jammed and I always find a place to park."

Before she finishes speaking, she whirls into an empty space with a Cadillac Escalade on one side and a Mercedes SUV on the other.

Mary stares in awe. "The people who drive these cars must be rich."

"Maybe."

The women walk through the mall window-shopping. Mary wears a jumper with sandals; Sasha wears a dress, and sports a cherry colored leather ankle boot.

Sasha eyes Mary, and proclaims, "You are a beautiful person; look at your reflection in the glass. Please understand this about yourself. Do not let others make you feel insecure or that they are better than you are. There are many people who feel like you, so do not feel like you are all alone. There are many people enjoy making others feel bad about themselves. You have to understand who these people are. They come to you in many forms. I am here for you Mary. You have my phone number and you know where I live; call if you need me for anything especially when you get down and depressed."

"Thank you."

"Let's get something to eat. Where shall we feed our faces?" Sasha asks with a big smile. "No franchise restaurants."

They glance around and find an empty table on the lower level of the food court.

"Mary I have a plan on the horizon. My plan is to have a party; I would like you to help me pull it together. Please think about if you want to help."

"Are you kidding? I have never helped with giving a party. What will I need to do?"

"We will have plenty of time to plan and figure it out. The next time we get together, we will start planning just make sure to clear it with your mom."

∞

Mary goes home considering what Sasha asked of her and at the same time excited to help and scared to ask her mom if she can help with a party.

What will I say to her? She is going to say no. I'm twenty six years old, so I'm going to ask.

The phone rings. Sasha asks, "Mary, have you talked to your mom about the party; what did she say?"

"I think she will be okay with it; she likes you."

Mary continues with a three-way call, "Mom, can I have a party? Sasha plans to have a party and wants me to help. She knows I need to get your permission."

Ms. Sutton hesitates. She answers, "Yes, I don't see why not."

"I love you mom."

∞

Two days later on Friday evening Raimee says to Lakeeda, "Let's go to a party; I feel good today."

"Wow girl, that's what I want to hear. What are you going to wear? You know you only have those work clothes."

"Frumpy, huh," Raimee responds with a laugh.
They both laugh.

"I have plenty of outfits you can choose from. Come over to my house."

With a gleam in her eye Raimee poses, "I'll probably need you to help me decide on something. Okay, what time?"

"I have a couple places to go first, so come over in about two hours and you can pick an outfit. You can dress at my place."

∞

Later that evening Lakeeda and Raimee arrive at what Raimee calls, "The most happening party around tonight."

"What is the name of this place?" Lakeeda asks. "I hope we can talk in here."

"Don't you worry, just come in, and let your hair down. We will talk, but first let's have some fun."

"I have not been in a club in six years. I feel a little out of place."

The appearance on her face and her saying, "I feel out of place," let it be known she is not a party girl.

Raimee heads for the dance floor and takes Lakeeda's arm to guide her. As they dance to a fast song, a handsome fellow approaches Lakeeda. He talks to her and all the while gazes at Raimee. Lakeeda gives Raimee the eye and shrugs her shoulder, as if to say what is up with this guy.

As both make it back to their seats, a voice says, "Both of you were jamming on the dance floor. May I buy you ladies a drink?" he asks with confidence.

"No thanks," Raimee responds.

"I don't drink," Lakeeda replies.

The guy smiles and hands Raimee a piece of paper as he walks away.

She opens the paper. Scribbled on the note are the name Ryan and a phone number.

"Are you happy with the work you do?" Lakeeda asks.

Raimee folds the note and stuffs it in her purse. "I've put so much time, devotion, and loyalty into that organization. With all the terrible headaches, nightmares, and voices I hear, I am really disabled and unable to function on most other jobs. I've been there five years; I guess I should be happy and feel lucky to have a job."

"Why do you say it like that? There you go. You are putting yourself down. You told me other people put you down enough."

"Yes," Raimee agrees, in a passive woe am I tone.

"So why are you doing it to yourself? There is no need to help others downgrade you. Tell me about you. What are the reasons you are working there?"

"I have to work; bills need to be paid. I like the idea of the type of job I have. I prefer to stay with what I know instead of dealing with other people. It is not so much the learning of a new job; it is more of dealing with new people that is keeping me from changing employers. Even though I'm not treated fairly where I'm at it's not worth the additional headache to start at the bottom and wade through the bull at a new job."

"Sasha is trying to help me find a different job where I help others and is looking for something else for Mary. She informs me of job postings, job lists, and job fairs. She says it can be a good opportunity to find different employment, and she volunteered to help Mary fill out applications. I called her and said, let's do it!"

Later her text to Sasha, "Around 6:00 p.m., I will stop by your house."

∞

"Come in," Sasha says, as Mary knocks on the door. "Can I get you something to drink? Would you like some nachos or fruit? Have a seat and relax; you don't have to work or worry when you're around me."

"Can we talk? I need someone to listen to me. I do not have anybody at all outside my immediate family who cares for me in a loving way. At times I need a friend, someone who will listen and not judge me; someone that I can tell things I'm not comfortable discussing with family."

Sasha asks with the aim of Mary revealing, "Do you know your friends? Who are the people that you spend time with other than your mom and brothers? Do you trust them?"

Mary gives her a *Thank You* for being there for me card. "You are my best friend. I can tell you anything.

"Raimee is a very good friend also. She is a professional. We get along and have things in common. She has migraines every day and her body aches all the time. Raimee and I are such good friends because many people (including the ones she works with) do not treat her best. They look at her with very little respect. We talk all the time about how this has made her feel throughout her life. I have four other friends I have met through my meetings. I'm not sure who I can trust other than my family, you, and Raimee."

Sasha continues, "Why do you trust Raimee?"

"She has a good heart and she's been downed through-out her life. There is something about her that feels trustworthy in the same way I'm able to trust you."

"Keep your heart guarded. How do you know she won't hurt you the way others have?"

"I truly believe in her. She is honest and really cares about me. Raimee treats people good, buying personal products for at least two to three other people every few weeks from her own money. These things she does for people that she does not brag or tell others. She does it because of her kind heart, yet her co-workers, bosses, and the men she deals with in her personal life misunderstand and mistreat her. People have hurt and wronged a really good person."

∞

She cries out of the clear blue and says, "I just feel so alone. I wish GOD would send me a mate to have my back on this earth. We both are alike in many ways including things that happen and the way people treat us. Raimee is kind, contrary to most of the people she encounters. They are fakers."

ORGANIZATION

S taff comes and goes all the time. Turnover seems inevitable. Some organizations and business industries are more prone to employee turnover than others are. A new woman walks the halls at Newhurst, Inc. with a smile on her face. She is on her way to the conference room; she is going to the same place Raimee is going. The monthly staff meeting is getting under way.

Mr. Martin, the CEO announces, "We have a new addition to our staff family. Please welcome Bailey Latiste."

"Hi Bailey, welcome Bailey, Ms. Bailey welcome, hello Ms. Bailey, hello, welcome, hi, Ms. Bailey welcome; glad to have you on the team," is heard respectively from Greg, Alicia, Theresa, Lionel, Dean, Breton, Dillon, Raimee, and Tareice.

"Thanks everybody, the feeling is mutual. I look forward to working with each of you."

Raimee sits at the table with eyes set on a few of her co-workers. Tareice is one of them. She never says anything out of the way or expresses her true feelings to her peers or bosses.

After returning to her office Raimee picks up her ringing cell phone, "Hello, I'm so glad you called. We had a meeting and I just want to snap. I can't take these people here much longer."

"That damn Tareice is a two-faced troublemaker. She thrives on repeating everybody's business. All she does is talk about each staff member behind their back and then act like she's oh so cushy and friends with each of them."

Raimee emphasizes, "I want to just blurt it out. Tareice shot my feelings with her nasty little trouble making lips going in your ear. You need to watch yourself. She is a manipulative, lying, troublemaker and she knows how to make you believe she is a sweet friend who will do anything for you. She acts this way with everyone."

∞

Bailey and Raimee attend most meetings at the same time.

"Raimee," Bailey shares, "I notice how the Leadership staff plays childish roles during the meeting. They laugh and giggle among themselves as if it is always an inside joke. I also notice during this and other meetings your superiors are never satisfied with the amount of work you perform. Your superior never has a kind word or compliment to give you. I also notice how every other manager receives kudos repeatedly. I usually keep things to myself and never say anything to you or anybody else."

Raimee knows her only as her new co-worker Bailey. She asks, "Why do you want to work here?"

"Well, I need to make some money and your organization is hiring. What's the problem?"

"I do not have a problem. I'm just thinking about when I will see your true colors."

"Come on now. What are you talking about?"

"Everybody is two-faced and I cannot take it. As a new person starts they too become part of the clique and show their true selves."

∞

Bailey sits in Tareice's office; both are talking and laughing. When Raimee walks in, both ladies look at each other and quickly pick up folders as if to be working.

"Ms. Raimee what can I do for you?" Tareice's trouble making ass asks.

Raimee wonders if there is a pattern. Is Bailey falling into the same trap all the rest have?

CONFESSIONS

Mary caresses her stomach at home in her room; she sits on the bed stretching her body to the right, stretching her body to the left.

She thinks to herself. *I am feeling funny. Somehow, there is a strange feeling going on inside me. This feeling is happening too much. I need someone to help me. I have to talk to someone about this, and soon.*

She wants to confront Raimee. She feels comfortable she is trustworthy enough to tell what is happening to her and rings her phone.

Raimee answers, "Hey, how are you doing? How are your headaches lately? Mine are worse."

"Raimee," Mary interrupts with the quickness. "I need to talk with you about something. I know what I am about to say will sound crazy. I don't know anybody else to talk to about this. I have not talked to my doctor, my psychiatrist, or my mom. So what I am about to say please don't tell anybody else."

Mary hesitates.

"What is it, Mary? What's wrong?"

"Okay, listen to this. For months I have beliefs there is something inside me."

"What?" Raimee asks with a puzzling look. "Something is going on?"

"I just want this feeling to leave my body," Mary continues. "If I talk to someone about this and explain the symptoms and how I feel I will be considered crazy; oh I mean more crazy. I know there is something going on inside me. Should I request they return me back to the crazy house?

"Something is happening to me different from the voices I normally hear."

Raimee observing wide-eyed Mary responds, "No you don't sound crazy. You want to know why?"

"Why?"

In a defining moment, Raimee reveals, "Because I feel the same way, having unfamiliar feelings inside my body. I've been feeling this way for some time."

"Oh wow, how long have your feelings been different? What does it feel like to you?"

Raimee tries to explain, "Mary, all I can tell you is its different and weird. Let us meet. We need to discuss this in person, not on the phone. What are you doing right now? I can pick you up and we can talk about it."

"Yes," before Raimee can finish the question. "Come get me now. We can go wherever you want."

"Let me get some clothes on and I'll see you in about one hour."

∞

After Raimee picks Mary up at her house, they go to The Cafe. The Cafe is a quiet, slightly dim lit place, where people congregate in a peaceful, significantly harmonious atmosphere–its twenty minutes from Mary's house.

"Would you like to order a drink?" the server asks.

Mary orders a Pepsi and Raimee orders a glass of wine.

Raimee declares, "Girl I need to unwind."

Mary responds, "Thank you for being my friend. I like this place; I feel good in here."

"I want to say thanks to you also. I love you as a friend."

"You are the only person who understands me. I can't talk to my family. Don't get me wrong, they love me, but they don't understand everything. I should thank you more than you thank me. I'm the one with the crazy problems," Mary expresses.

Raimee continues pouring out heartfelt words, "We have a connection and a bond. I do not understand why, but it makes me happy."

"GOD, my family, and my job are the only things that matter to me in life. I yearn for someone to take problems home to when things are unbalanced. GOD has to bear being the ears all the time. Two of my three items are not in balance and I cannot take it any longer. Add on to that this crazy weirdness going on inside that I can't do anything about."

Raimee cries, "I'm so helpless, so unhappy."

∞

"Okay Raimee, tell me what it feels like to you. What kind of weird way are you feeling?"

"I always hear voices and noises in my head (yet I am not considered to have schizophrenia), but now the voices are somehow different from usual. To tell the truth it feels like an alien. I do not know any other way to explain it. If something strange and weird is going on inside of me I want to know what it is. My head hurts constantly; it is hurting as we speak. There are nonstop vibrations. I hear voices, but as always, I cannot make out a word said.

"The voices do not hurt; they are usually gibberish, sounds, and words that do not make sense. They give the weirdest feeling I have ever felt."

"That is exactly the way my body feels," Mary agrees.

Raimee places her hand on top of Mary's head, "Why is this happening to us? You know that sometimes I just want to give up. Life is so hard. Dealing with a chronic illness and continually experiencing job and relationship unhappiness keeps me miserable all the time."

Raimee and Mary discuss it and both come to the same conclusion. Each has an unknown presence they do not understand. They know they want whatever is within them to leave their bodies.

How?

DOCTOR CONSULT

Raimee concludes, "We are in agreement to contact both our doctors for immediate appointments. We need to make it sound like we're a danger to ourselves so we can get a quicker appointment."

"Yes, and I hope we both can be seen soon," Mary agrees.

"I am going to wait until I hear something from my doctor as to what is wrong before I discuss it with my son, Byron."

∞

Collaboratively Dr. Percy, Mary's doctor and Dr. Jahn, Raimee's doctor consult to determine if they warrant research specialist referrals to the Mid West Hospital and Research Facility located in Texas.

Dr. Percy says, "Dr. Jahn, I'll have my office schedule the referrals and testing setup for both ladies. It's important the specialists understand the reason for testing the ladies together is to compare everything including tests, medications, all procedures, all outcomes, and both ladies responses–physical, mental, and emotional."

"Hello, Mid West Hospital and Research Facility. May I help you?"

"This is Melissa with Dr. Percy's office. Dr. Sean Percy and Dr. Oliver Jahn need immediate scheduling, both at the same time for Mary Sutton and Raimee Alexander."

"What is the reason for scheduling?" the clerk asks.

"Both Ms. Mary Sutton and Ms. Raimee Alexander will be tested to find out what is happening in their bodies."

"Hold on for a date."

"How about April 12th?" the Mid West Scheduling clerk asks as she types in the computer for the new appointment scheduling screen.

"Okay," Melissa replies. "What are the procedures and the information necessary to provide the patients?"

"Letters will be sent by mail tomorrow. Each woman is to report to the Mid West Hospital and Research Facility on April 12th, no later than 10 a.m. They should prepare to spend at least two weeks. Family members, a maximum of three per patient are welcome to support their loved one. Food is not included; travel and lodging is included for the entire stay. The letter and paperwork sent to Raimee and Mary lists all information. It's only January 28th, so there is enough time before the hospital date prepare personal and work arrangements if necessary. Please mail back the information packet by March 20th."

∞

Raimee and Mary plan to get both families together and break the news.

Friday evening, 7:00 p.m., Raimee and her son Byron meet at the Sutton's house.

"Everybody to the living room; please have a seat. Raimee and I have something to discuss with you."

Bobby responds, "What is it? Come on tell us, talk to us."

Ms. Sutton utters under her breath, "Oh my GOD!"

Bobby and Malcolm glare at each other. Malcolm's eyes squint, lips purse, and nostrils flare.

"I will start," Raimee exclaims, as she scoots to the edge of the couch. "Mary and I have been experiencing some weird sensations in our bodies for some time.

"We both are patients of doctors who determined the issue is serious enough to warrant studying us at a research facility. They are scheduling both of us as in-patients at the Mid West Hospital and Research Facility located in Texas."

"When does this take place?" Ms. Sutton asks.

"We are to be at the facility by 10:00 a.m. on April 12th, and it's going to be quite a long drive," Mary explains.

"Tell us more," placing his hands together as a gentle request, Byron insists. "Give all the details."

"We can bring up to three family members for each of us. They will provide lodging and travel. We must provide the food for our family members. Mary and I will eat as part of the hospital stay. Our doctors told us to expect to be gone approximately two weeks. We will need to get our affairs straight with our employers, family members, and schools as necessary."

∞

February 5th, Raimee and Mary are at their doctors. They are together for updates on their expected hospital stay at Mid West Hospital and Research Facility.

"Did you bring the letter sent by the Facility?" asks Dr. Jahn.

Pulling the letter from her purse, "Yes we did. It states we should be there no later than 10 a.m., April 12th. Since it appears we have similar issues, they want the both of us to test together for monitoring and comparisons. After all the testing is complete, the results will be relayed to you.

"Dr. Jahn," Raimee continues. "Please, inform us of the outcomes as soon as possible. Whatever the diagnosis, I want to know immediately. I cannot take this feeling inside of me; it is an undeniably weird sensation. We are appreciative and want to thank you looking out for us, scheduling our trip, and assisting with family accommodations at Midwest.

"My son will accompany me."

Mary says, "My mother and younger brother will go with me. I'm so happy, because I don't want to do this without my family. I love my mom and brothers and they love me. They want the best for me and always say they hope something will come along to help me. Did you know that the Midwest Hospital & Research Facility in Texas pays for everything except food? They will pay the testing, research, travel for all, and a place to stay for the family."

Ms. Sutton announces as if she is proud, "My baby's going to the well renowned Mid West Hospital and Research Facility located in Texas."

Dr. Jahn informs them, "As a reminder in preparation to be away, I suggest you discuss this with your places of employment to see what they need to do. Are you able to keep your job? One important thing is that you need to be clear with them and get a good understanding of how this absence will affect your employment."

∞

Eagerness is turning into anticipation. Two weeks before the trip, Mary and Ms. Sutton begin packing.

Mary suggests to her mom, "You will need to pack more stuff than me. I will be in hospital clothes. Wonder if I can use my own soap, shampoo, lotion, and stuff. Make sure to get all your meds and refills before we leave."

Both Mary and Raimee are getting braids for minimal maintenance. Ms. Sutton is getting a fresh perm; and Malcolm is going to the barber a few days before departing.

∞

Raimee tells Lakeeda, "Annette, my co-worker asks if she can help get my work in order, if I need help filing." She states, "It's to help you stress less while you are away."

"I was in sheer amazement. All these years I have complained about the workload and the need for help with filing and, they turned a deaf ear, with no assistance. Now I get volunteer help, although, the same co-workers said I must be incompetent. People are something else. I am so sick of the shit and crap that people have given me throughout the years. I have kept my mouth closed because I need the work, I know not to express the pain and suffering I feel, and the constant unfairness and mistreatment inflicted upon me from my current and past employers. All this stresses me out."

MIDWEST

Mary and Raimee together with Ms. Sutton, Malcolm, and Byron as support, travel together by rental car to the Midwest Hospital and Research Facility. Byron and Ms. Sutton take turns driving. It is a thirteen hour drive and neither one of them are the best long distance drivers. Switching off every two hours works better and allows everyone to utilize the facilities.

Byron exclaims, "We should get there by 8:00 a.m. We left at 6:00 p.m. last evening and this makes our third stop. We are making good time and I am on track for the travel time with an estimated six stops. So buckle up because we're half the way there."

∞

Byron pulls up in front of Mid West and parks. Located in front of the hospital a sign reveals Valet parking available - $14.00.

Viewing the sign, he considers aloud, sighs and declares, "Yeah right. I told you all we would make it here on time. Its 7:40 a.m. and I estimated around eight. We are scheduled to be here at 10:00 a.m. so we're good my ladies."

He walks inside the facility and requests of the medical assistant, "Please let them know there are two women out here in the same vehicle scheduled to be admitted to the hospital. Thank you."

In less than five minutes, Mary and Raimee greet attendants with wheelchairs.

Byron whips the car into gear and heads toward the hospital-parking garage. The fee is $6.50 for all day parking. *That $14.00 is ridiculous.*

"Please have a seat and we'll take you to registration for check in."

Attendants wheel both Mary and Raimee to the check in window for in-patient registration. Mary is at window A, and Raimee is at window D. These financial counselors determine the necessary insurance and payment arrangements.

Ms. Sutton verbally expresses legitimate concern, "This should have been taken care of before we arrived. What about the paperwork for pre-registration mailed out previously? They are just wasting time. It took long enough for us to get here. Why should we sit in a registration office half the morning?

"Ma'am how much longer? We all have to use the bathroom including the ladies you're registering."

"Oh, I am not quite sure, until we finish. Each of you can take a turn. The women's restroom is four doors down on the right and the men's restroom is five doors on the left. We don't mind waiting while the ladies relieve themselves."

Mary declares, "Me first, I can't hold it any longer. Mom, will you take me? That way we both can go at the same time and get back to pre-registering."

"Sure baby, come on, let us go real quick. You know I can't hold my water very long."

After Mary and Raimee finish in the bathroom and return to work out arrangements with the financial counselors, attendant orders are to pick up both ladies. Counselors place a band on Mary and Raimee's arm containing their name, birth date, and doctor's information.

The attendants inquire, "Are you ready to go to your rooms now? It is easier and quicker to take you there instead of you trying to find the rooms by yourself. I don't want you nice young ladies to get lost in this big ole hospital."

"Okay fellas take them to the fourth floor; rooms are already prepared and ready for the two. Hold on just a minute so I can let you know exactly where to take them. Ms. Alexander is in room 415; Ms. Sutton is in room 410. Here is each of their paperwork; I am attaching to their wheelchairs. Check each in with the nurse's station after you have dropped them off."

∞

Attendants drop Mary off first; Raimee arrives at her room next. Both ladies have semi-private rooms.

"Mary Sutton, I will pull the curtain for you to get undressed. On your bed is a gown and pants. You can put on whichever pieces you want. Are you cold natured? If so, you can put both pieces on. I can also give you a robe if you did not bring one with you."

In Raimee's room, she finished dressing, and is lying on the bed, and scanning the TV. "I'm cold. Can you turn up the heat and give me some additional blankets?"

"Yes, would you like a heated blanket and a robe? I can give you an extra pillow also."

"Thank you for being so nice and helpful," Raimee replies. "I thought it would be hard–assuming you know what I mean. I was saying; I was assuming, which I should not have been doing. You have been really nice and accommodating."

"You are welcome. Lunch will be ready around noon. Even though you just arrived, I will bring you a tray. Eat what you want and leave what you do not. You can request a more specific menu when dietary picks up your tray. Make sure to ask them for the dietary menu form to fill out. Each day afterwards when your breakfast arrives, you will have a menu sheet included for the next day's breakfast, lunch, and dinner. If you want something specific to eat, I suggest you fill out by checking what you want for each mealtime. Lunch delivery is around noon and dinner around 5:30. Try to hand in the dietary menu sheet no later than the dinner pickup of each evening. If not they will bring you a default tray, whatever that is. If there's a food you prefer or prefer not to eat, this is a good way to let them know."

Raimee explains, "I can't drink orange or grapefruit juice and it's usually included on most trays. Therefore, I mark apple, cranberry, or grape juice on my slip."

The nurse informs her, "Your family can come in shortly until visiting hours are over."

"Which is at what time?"

"Eight o'clock is the last hour, Sunday through Thursday. Friday and Saturday hours are until 10:00 p.m. Please be sure to let your family know the times."

"Will you be sure to tell Mary and her family? Thanks so much.

"What is our schedule for procedures and anything else? Can Mary and I visit with each other? What about a curfew or ending time we must be back in our beds?"

"If your doctors have not given you a breakdown of scheduled procedures and a timeframe, you will need to talk with them. They are probably waiting after settling before coming to you with the details of your stay. I am sure they will discuss it with you and your family members. Okay?"

"I understand. Thanks. Oh, I would love something to drink since we will not eat for over one hour.

"I cannot wait for something to drink. I'm parched."

"What would you like? We have ginger ale, lemon-lime, and water; also there's an ice machine in the hallway."

"Ginger ale with ice in a cup would be nice. Are you both our nurse?"

"No, she has a different nurse. Her nurse will take care of her."

"It would be nice if Mary and I could share the same nurse; we are both here for the same thing. Do you think that is a great idea? Maybe I should suggest it to our doctor.

"Nurse how much longer before I can have a visit from my family?"

"Your blood pressure and some blood tests need taken. Someone will be here shortly to take your pressure and draw blood. Afterwards, if the doctor is okay with it and doesn't need to do anything else, I'll let your family come up."

∞

Byron walks in to Raimee's room, gives her a big hug, "I love you mom. How are you tonight?"

"Bored, but it is good rest. Has Ms. Sutton and Malcolm visited with Mary?"

"Yes, they are there now."

Byron turns around looks over the room and makes a 360-degree turn. "This is a nice room. Are you glad you're alone and don't have a roommate?"

"Yes, I'm glad, but I don't understand why they didn't put Mary and me in the same room."

∞

Ms. Sutton and Malcolm sit up close to Mary's bed.

Holding hands Ms. Sutton prays, "Thank you LORD, please hear my prayer. Walk with Mary and with Ms. Raimee in their time of need. In Jesus name we pray, AMEN."

She gets up, kisses Mary on the cheek. Malcolm also gives her a peck.

"I love both of you; I'm so glad you are here with me."

"This is a semi-private room. Why are you and Raimee not sharing this room?" Malcolm asks.

"I don't know."

A loud announcement over the intercom says, "Its 8 o'clock, visiting hours are now over. Please come back tomorrow. Thank you!"

"See you both tomorrow," Mary exclaims, as Ms. Sutton and Malcolm hug her at the same time.

∞

"Gotta go mom; I love you. See you tomorrow after you finish testing."

"All right son, I love you too. Goodnight."

∞

Next morning, around six-thirty the nurse enters Mary's room.

"Good morning, I'm here to take you for testing. Finish eating your breakfast; testing is around seven. Testing will also start around eight o'clock tomorrow morning. Do not eat or drink anything after midnight tonight.

"Raimee is eating eggs and drinking decaf coffee. She goes for testing at 7:30."

∞

Nurse on duty alerts Raimee, "Tests have been ordered for both you and Mary including multiple tests to scan different angles of your bodies. X-rays, CT scans, MRI's are all included. Please do not eat or drink after midnight tonight. Both of you will go for testing around 8:00 a.m. in the morning and you won't be able to eat or drink anything until after the testing is complete."

∞

Raimee and Mary move to an area where both receive rounds of x-rays, MRI's and blood tests at the same time. X-rays and MRI's on various parts of the body, including the brain, neck, lungs, spine, stomach, intestines, thoracic, clavicle, liver, and kidneys are currently on the testing list.

∞

Two weeks later Dr. Nowling and Dr. Herod meet for lunch in Dr. Herod's office.

Dr. Herod and Dr. Nowling briefly discuss their findings.

"Did you see anything?" Dr. Herod asks after reviewing each ladies chart.

"No I haven't; we have additional testing scheduled. Something will show up.

Dr. Herod what do you think? It is a mystery to me. I see a mass in each but I have no idea what it could be. I have never seen anything like it. Have you?"

"No. Is it necessary that we perform additional testing?"

Dr. Nowling responds, "Yes, I feel additional testing is required and necessary, but not from us and not at the Mid West facility. We will contact a facility with even more up to date technology for their testing and opinions. First, we will discuss with the doctors there and get their initial opinion. After that, we can pose the suggestions to Mary and Raimee for The Israel Medical Facility in Canada. Have the scheduling department from Midwest to contact The Israel Medical Facility right away. Give them my contact information and yours as secondary. Are you okay with that?"

"Yes of course," is Dr. Herod's immediate answer. "I don't have a problem with you being the lead contact."

∞

Mary and Raimee move back to their rooms.

Dr. Nowling discusses medical issues with each family, "We have seen something on the scans but have no idea what it is."

Ms. Sutton is eager to know, "What are the plans now? Since you don't know what it is, can you perform some type of surgery to find out?"

"We can discuss it with the Mid West Research Facility doctors and upon their recommendations let you know and give our opinion. The best thing now is to inform Mary and Raimee. Once we hear something definitive, we can share what we hear with you all."

Ms. Sutton agrees, "Okay," with hope in her eyes.

"Bring the ladies in; we are ready to share with everyone. They already know the basics.

"Mary and Raimee, you know that results from the testing determine a foreign presence, but unknown as to what it is. Do you all understand that? Right now after the initial testing, we have only determined a 100% fact that something is there. It appears to be the same type of foreign presence in both of you.

"The results are why we are contemplating sending the both of you for additional testing to another facility. This facility is even more sophisticated than Midwest and the doctors are some of the most knowledgeable in the field."

∞

"Why didn't they initially refer them to the better facility?

"Why were we told Midwest is a more sophisticated facility and didn't or couldn't find out what is wrong? We traveled for thirteen hours to get here. We don't know any more now than was known before we came."

REFERRAL

D r. Nowling and Dr. Herod sit down with both Raimee and Mary.

"After testing and consultation the decision is to refer both of you to a parasitic and infectious disease research department. The Israel Medical Center located in Canada welcomes both of you for the additional testing we feel is required. Dr. Herod and I are certain that the answers we seek will not be available without this testing. The Israel Medical Center has the equipment and expertise needed to do more in depth testing and research studies. It is their specialty.

"How do you feel about going Mary?"

"I am ready. I want to find out what's wrong with me."

"The same here," Raimee expresses. "Just let me know when and how to get there. I guess the next step is to explain everything to us in more detail and to inform our family."

"When can we tell our families? My mom will be beside herself to know I'll be heading to Canada for some more tests. Can you give us a little more detail and then we can discuss it with them?"

"Of course," Dr. Nowling, Mary's doctor explains. "It will probably take an additional stay of three to four weeks. Both of you will go for testing at the same time that will include a battery of tests that are more sophisticated and technologically advanced. I suggest you report to work until the Canada trip. Get all your work and personal affairs in as much order as possible. Discuss your work options with your employer, especially who will be able to do your work while you are gone. Make sure they are aware it could be for at least one month.

"Carlina, please contact Mary's mother, Ms. Sutton, Raimee and her son, Byron. Schedule a date for a call in appointment so we can explain next steps. Schedule both families at the same time for a conference call."

∞

July 20th Dr. Herod walks in Dr. Nowling's office. Ms. Sutton, Mary, Raimee, and Byron receive three-way conference calls.

"Ms. Sutton and Byron we need to discuss Mary and Raimee's proposed medical plans. There is a need for additional testing. Although, the additional testing is not required it is necessary to our continued efforts in figuring out the cause of the issues plaguing them. Both of them understand the explanations. As soon as we get the go ahead from both families, we will proceed further. Preliminary arrangements are to transport both women to the Israel Medical Facility in Canada. It is a reputable and distinguished hospital with modern, state of the art equipment, and groundbreaking research and technique studies. We already discussed it with Mary and Raimee. Both say it is a go. Both women request we explain the new plans and give you the details of the trip.

"This trip will require air flight to Canada, with a stop or two before reaching the medical facility. Each woman can bring three family members. For this hospital stay, all expenses will be taken care of including travel, lodging, and food at the facility (three meals per day per family member).

"We are discussing their cases and brief medical history with the necessary staff at The Israel Medical Center. The physician in charge agrees that sending both of them there is the best thing. No discussions have been made of their full medical and other history. Once Mary and Raimee give their okay, discussions with the family can begin.

"Even though it is their body and their decisions, both always make it known that family is very important and we respect that. We understand the need to have family commit to you in times like these.

"It is critical that we let The Israel Medical Center know as soon as possible of Mary and Raimee's decision to move forward with the testing. Logistics will be in place specifically to accommodate the testing we feel is necessary for them.

"Once the facility knows of their plans to proceed, someone from IMC will begin the process of scheduling everything from the hospital stay to air flight, and lodging arrangements and designation and preparation on the fifth floor of the hospital.

"You are probably saying to yourself why would a hospital go through all of this for the two of them. Am I right?"

Byron stares suspiciously at both doctors and inquires, "Exactly, why would they go through all of it for mom and Mary?"

"It's really quite simple Byron; it is important to find out what's going on with them and why this is happening to the both of them at the same time. This is why hospitals and facilities like The Israel Medical Center exist.

"Plans are to work with both women at the same time. This will allow the medical staff the ability to monitor and compare treatment and outcomes. We are thankful to have somewhere to send people who have unexplained illnesses or ailments that local hospitals and doctors are not able to diagnose, treat, or find a cure.

"All necessary and required equipment, tools, and imaging will install, prior to their arrival. They will have a set of medical personnel dedicated to them, essential only personnel not only for their comfort but also for their testing and safety. It is a private area with two beds placed side by side allowing enough distance between them in the event Raimee or Mary needs to be cared for separately, if something goes wrong, if there is a reaction with one and the other is not involved, or within too close a distance. Duplicates of all the equipment for each woman assures there is two of everything. The only thing Raimee and Mary share is the room and the TV. Actually, I am not sure about the TV. There's a possibility each lady has her own TV with sound remote."

"I can ask about the TV," Mary remarks. "If I have company or Raimee has company we can keep occupied with our own TV with remote sound and not have to interfere or interrupt the other persons channel preference. That makes sense, Huh?"

"I'm asking if both families can let me know as soon as possible which family members plan to accompany each patient to Canada."

"When is the schedule date for testing?" Malcolm asks. "I know I don't talk much, but finding out what's wrong with my Sis is high priority."

Ms. Sutton eyes Malcolm, with a big smile and reaches her arms out for a hug.

∞

"Again, as I have stated, I wish they were referred to the medical facility with advanced knowledge and better outcomes first. Missing work at different times could negatively affect their employment."

EMPLOYER LOYALTY

D r. Nowling continues, "I don't have a date for you to plan but should have a date finalized no later than two days after I'm able to give the doctors a definitive answer as to whether both ladies will be present. If okay with all of you, I can inform them tomorrow and should know something with specific dates by end of the week. For now, you should plan for the trip to take place in approximately four to six weeks, and you should expect to be gone up to four weeks.

"Mary and Raimee please clear it with your places of employment. Be as truthful and upfront as possible. This way there will not be any surprises on the part of the women or their employer's expectations. It is very important they work out the details of the leave from employment with their superiors as soon as possible. I hope that everything works out for both of you and neither loses their job over this additional testing.

"As soon as you discuss the additional need for testing with your employer please make contact to let us know what is said and of your continued interest in participating. Dr. Nowling or myself will be more than happy, if necessary, to speak with your employer."

"Okay," Raimee responds. "I can only imagine what my employer says. My job is critical because there are not many who can do what I do. We just lost one employee and the other employee left last year. That leaves yours truly to step in and fulfill all the roles. It's truly a one woman show."

Mary remarks with uneasiness, "I'll let you know as soon as I talk to my boss. I hope they can get someone from another shift to move over temporarily, or at least get someone from another store to fill in until my return. It should not be a problem; I'll let you know something as soon as I find out."

∞

Mary discusses her health needs and plans with her employer. "Mrs. Burns, I have a special request. Due to major health issues, I am requesting four weeks off work. I also need to request FMLA. Thanks."

Mrs. Burns, to Mary's surprise asks, as if concerned, "When will you need to be off?"

"I'm not sure yet; we are in the planning stages and trying to get things worked out. I will let you know as soon as I find out.

"Right now, they told me to ask of the possibility of getting off work in four to six weeks for up to four weeks. Please give me an answer as soon as possible so I can tell the doctors. They will then be able to move forward.

She heads to the back room and begins to make a call on her cell phone, "Hey mom, I talked to my boss today. She will give me an answer soon; although, I don't know when. Okay, I'm going; I've got to tell Raimee before I get back to working."

∞

The next day Raimee goes to her Director. "Mr. Townsend, may I speak with you for about ten minutes?"

"Okay Raimee, come in."

"Mr. Townsend, I'm experiencing a major health issue and will be involved in some research and testing. Due to this I need to request approximately four weeks off, probably sometime in a couple of months. I will also need to request the FMLA program. Thanks for listening; I hope to hear an answer from you soon, as my doctor needs to continue planning the procedures."

"Yes, I can do that. Thanks."

Within minutes of returning to her desk, Mary's phone rings. "Hello."

"Mary, this is Raimee. I talked to my boss just minutes ago. Have you spoken to yours?"

"Yeah, I finished letting her know and will be waiting on her answer."

"Mine didn't give me an answer either."

"Did you request the FMLA program like I suggested?"

"I did. Thank you for providing the information to ask my employer."

∞

"Let me talk to you later Mary; my boss is coming."

"Sure."

"Raimee, I'm thinking over what you told me. Four weeks is a long time to be off. Who will you find to perform your job duties?"

"I'll work something out Mr. Townsend."

"What, how are you going to work out something? Someone needs to be on the job. As I stated, four weeks is a long time. Wow!

"If you absolutely need to be off, I cannot stand in the way of your health. You must show someone the things that must be taken care of the four weeks you will be off."

"Yes, I can do that. Thanks again."

CANADA BOUND

T he day is finally here for Mary, Raimee, Ms. Sutton, Malcolm, and Raimee's son, Byron to board the flight to Canada. Only Raimee has experience flying in an airplane. Raimee and Byron arrive at the airport around 7:15 a.m. After checking their luggage and passing through the security checkpoint, they are heading toward Gate 35.

"It's like a shopping mall mom. Did you forget to tell me the airport was so nice? We are at Gate 15 and still need to get to Gate 35. Wow, my legs are gonna be worn out."

"You are a young man; you have those young legs. I'm sure you will be good."

"Awe, I am just kidding. How long is the flight?"

"Look at your ticket, it will list the departure time and the arrival time."

"The departure time is 8:50 a.m.; the arrival time is 3:55 p.m. We're gonna be on a plane for seven hours? Seven hours is a long time. What if we have to use the restroom before landing?"

"Use it before you leave. If you need to use it before we get to our destination there is a bathroom on the plane."

"Are you for real?"

"Look at the ticket again. We have one stop to change flights. The ticket shows we arrive in Chicago around 10:20 a.m. and our connecting flight leaves for Canada at 12:30 p.m., so we have a two-hour layover in Chicago. That will give us enough time to use the restroom, get something to eat if we want, and get to the connecting flight."

"There are the Sutton's. Hey Mary, Ms. Sutton, and Malcolm. How long have you all been waiting?" Byron asks.

Malcolm responds as if he cannot wait to complain, "We've been here since 6:30 this morning, and I'm sleepy and tired already. We came a little early because mom was worried we would miss the plane."

Ms. Sutton in agreement responds, "I am. Since this is my first flight, I did not know how long it would take or what to expect. This trip is very important. Mary needs to be in Canada on time for her testing procedures," she chuckles. "So sue me for being extra cautious and wanting to be here in plenty of time."

"According to the ticket, around 4:00 p.m. we'll be landing in Canada," Mary explains.

"Good morning Raimee and Byron; are you woke or is it still a little too early? Did you grab a bite to eat? I think we will get something, maybe a breakfast sandwich."

Ms. Sutton continues, "I'm going to get something that can be fixed quick and take it back to the gate. Let us stay together; we can order now, if you want something. Once we find our gate and seating, we can take turns going to the restroom. Raimee, you should go first, then Mary and so on."

"What about the mall like atmosphere?" Byron asks. "It's crazy but nice. Look Mary, at the nice things for sell inside this airport. There are a lot of different shops and restaurants. I thought only planes flew in and out of an airport. It is like a mini mall. Come look at this kiosk with all kinds of jewelry."

Walking toward the gates, restaurants galore come into view.

Raimee says in a delightful tone, "Look at the handbag kiosk. Wow, there are so many different styles. Oh my goodness, it is like heaven."

"Why is this store called a kiosk?" Mary asks.

Raimee is happy to explain, "Because it's not inside walls. It is set up in the hallway of the mall.

"Who's ready to fly?"

"I am ready, so ready. I'm cool and I know what to expect. It will be easy breezy."

"Mary, how do you know what to expect? You've never been on a plane either," Malcolm heckles.

"I'm just that kinda girl. I have seen people riding flights on TV. It's a breeze, no reason to be afraid. All you have to do is relax, sit back, and take a nap. You'll be there before you know it."

Raimee shares some experience, "I like to bring my laptop or some type of device and watch a movie while the plane is in flight. I am also in agreement with Mary; a good nap is always welcome. The only thing is you can't watch a movie until the pilot gives permission for the use of electronic devices."

∞

Ten-eighteen in the morning, the plane safely arrives in Chicago, the layover airport. Raimee tries to keep everyone together, so they can eat, use the restroom, and go through the gate for Canada.

∞

Its 12:00 p.m., everyone ate, used the restroom, and made it through check-in. The announcement for the connecting flight to Canada boarded at Gate 35.

∞

Now it is 3:40 p.m.; the pilot has several announcements. The plane lands at the Canadian airport in ten minutes. Sit in your seat, and shut off all electronic devices.

Raimee closes her laptop and places it in the bag. "We are here."

The plane arrives and comes to a stop.

∞

Malcolm laughingly recalls, as everyone waits for luggage at the baggage claim, "You all should have seen the look on your faces as we took off. Mary, I know you said it would be easy breezy, but the look on your face was priceless. I should have taken a pic, cause Miss Thang, you look scared also."

"Sorry, I do not believe it and even if I did, you don't have a way to prove it. No pic, no proof."

"Bam," Malcolm bears proof, as he shows Mary a pic of herself on his camera. "Now what did you say?"

"You rotten little turd. Why would you take a picture of me? Don't show that to anybody.

She reaches for his phone, "I'm gonna get your phone and delete that.

"To be serious how far is the hospital and how will we get there?" she continues.

"There is supposed to be a shuttle bus waiting for us. It was pre-arranged as part of the hospital stay," Raimee responds. "Byron, you and Malcolm please check on the shuttle. There is an information desk right up front; look for the sign. Find out where the Israel Medical Facility picks up, and what time."

"I need to use the bathroom before we load on the shuttle. Ms. Sutton will you watch the luggage? When I return you and Mary can go. The boys can go as soon as they return."

They need a full row of seats to accommodate both families. Ms. Sutton is keeping a watchful eye on both sides including directly in front of her.

Raimee cannot wait. She heads toward the bathroom. With a sigh of relief, "Thank GOD, there's a short line."

Byron leads the way to the shuttle stop. He searches for the bus they need through all the other shuttles and cabs lurking around. "I see the shuttle sign," he calls out. "We'll wait over there until it comes."

"Will we have seats to sit on?" Ms. Sutton asks in a concerned voice.

Ms. Sutton, Raimee, and Mary squeeze on the small bench located directly in front of the shuttle stop sign. Five minutes pass, ten minutes, and after twelve minutes a shuttle bus labeled Israel Medical Facility pulls up.

"Hello is everyone going to the Israel Facility?" the little driver asks.

"Yes," Ms. Sutton eagerly replies.

Looking as the driver loads the luggage onto the bus, Byron steps down to help, while everybody else loads on. It is a small travel bus; no other passengers, just the five of them.

"I love the way it looks here. We've been in Canada only one hour and I'm ready to move here."

Wrapping his arms around and kissing her cheeks, Byron says to his mom, "You want to move everywhere you visit."

She laughs, "Yeah darling, you're right. I guess I'm just tired of the same ole existence."

∞

Arriving at the Israel Medical Center, Dr. Prasont, Dr. Neson, and Dr. Gannt stand outside of the building waiting for them.

Dr. Neson slightly steps forward and he asks, "How was your flight?"

Ms. Sutton responds, "It's a first for all of us except Raimee. It was good; wish it was for a happy vacation and not a medical reason."

"Let us get formalities out of the way. I am Dr. Prasont, Mary's physician; this is Dr. Neson, Raimee's physician; and to my left, Dr. Gannt, Head of Parasitic and Infectious Research."

"Thank you, I am Raimee Alexander, and this is my son Byron."

"My name is Mary Sutton, along with my mother, Ms. Juanita Sutton and my brother, Malcolm."

Dr. Gannt remarks, "You have the tour Dr. Prasont."

"Thank you Dr. Gannt; we don't have enough time to tour the entire facility, but allow me to walk you through the wings where you'll be located during your stay."

Dr. Prasont walks the family around the facility. "Take the west wing elevator to the 5th floor. Turn to the corridor numbered 501-509–the study and research area scheduled for Mary and Raimee. You can see the equipment has been set up. Selective care of nurses, aides, and assistants will provide care exclusively for each of you.

"Mary and Raimee, nurses Asa and Lori will take you now to your rooms. Dr. Gannt will come through shortly to go over your testing schedule."

"Okay, let me say goodnight to my mom and brother and give them a hug.

"Love you both."

"Mary, we love you forever."

Raimee opens her arms.

Byron hugs her and plants a kiss on her face. "Love you mom."

"Love you more son."

∞

Advance arrangements are set up. Ms. Sutton, Malcolm and Byron go to the family visiting center where supportive family members stay during the entire trip. Since Byron is sixteen, he has a separate adjoining room, with a shared bath. The doors between the rooms remain unlocked and left open. Both families are okay with the arrangements.

Dr. Prasont informs the families, "Food is served buffet style daily until 7:00 p.m.

"Listed below on the flyer are time slots for the three major meals (buffet style only), Breakfast 6:00 a.m. to 9:00 a.m., Lunch 11:00 a.m. to 1:00 p.m., Dinner 5:00 to 7:00 p.m.

"Certain times of the day you may visit with Mary and Raimee.

"Both ladies will be picked up bright and early tomorrow morning for testing."

It is 8:30 p.m. and Dr. Gannt stops by, "Hello again ladies. I am here to give you some details of your testing schedule. Beginning tomorrow morning, you will receive a MRI scan of the brain. Other tests will be performed."

∞

Next morning attendants wheel both ladies to the pre-testing area.

"Here comes our family. Hurry and take a seat so we can talk. I'm kinda nervous; how about you Raimee?"

"Some, but GOD will see us through. Last night I prayed for both of our families and us. That is why I am not stressing too much.

"Please pray for us Ms. Sutton, Malcolm, and Byron."

As soon as Raimee asks them to pray, Dr. Prasont and Dr. Neson enter the room ready to start. Their facemasks and gloves are already on. "Good morning Ms. Alexander and Ms. Sutton; are you ready? Assisting us, we have nurses Linda Brazier for Raimee and Brandon Kelley for Mary. Again, remember we will be working with both of you at the same time.

"First, we are going to start by taking both of you to the room where you will be at for the initial testing. Next, we will do an MRI. Dr. Prasont, Dr. Gannt, and I will review and determine next action steps.

"If you are ready, let's go. Your families will be in the waiting area. It is somewhat comfortable with lounging chairs, a microwave, coffee pot, snack and soda machine, and a sandwich vending machine. Don't forget family that daily, breakfast, lunch, and dinner is available to each of you at no charge. Give the checkout your name and room number."

Mary softly says, "Bye mom and Malcolm; I'll be back real soon."

Ms. Sutton throws a few alternating hand kisses, "We love you."

Raimee tells her son, "See you later and love you always."

"Love you too mom."

∞

Aides take the women to Radiology for several tests. The room is set up with two identical MRI stations.

"Please take off your upper clothing and slip this gown on," the technician requests. "Do you have anything in your hair, hairpins or other holders?"

"No we don't," Mary replies, as she nods at Raimee for approval of her answer.

"You can change behind the curtain while I step out of the room."

"I've never had x-rays or MRI's before," Mary expresses. "Will it hurt at all? I'm kinda nervous."

"No, it won't hurt," Raimee says in a calming voice. "Just move and stand the way the technician requests of you. An MRI is a little different than X-rays, but never hurts."

"Do not say it is different Raimee. You are getting me worried." Mary scopes the room for equipment. "There is two of everything just like they said."

Advance arrangements are set up. The clock on the wall shows 8:45 a.m.

"It's time to take your blood pressure now." Linda cuffs Raimee and Brandon cuffs Mary. Both write notes in respective files.

∞

Ten o'clock a.m. Ms. Sutton stands up and approaches Byron and Malcolm, "Hold on to my purse while I go to the vending machines. What would each of you like?"

"I can go for a snack and a drink; I'll take a bag of regular potato chips and a citrus drink."

"I want a bag of barbecue chips and water."

"Okay, I should be back in about fifteen minutes. Make sure to keep your ears peeled for any updates."

Malcolm pulls out his gaming system, set up to play an online basketball game. "Do you play?"

"Yeah I play some."

"You want to play me so I can kick your booty," Malcolm brags.

"Don't go there, don't try to act like I'm old; I'm only five months older than you."

Ms. Sutton returns with the snacks as the young men play on the game.

"Here you go; two bags of chips, water, and a citrus drink. Enjoy!

"It is 10:15 a.m. While you boys play the game, I am going to rest on this recliner. Please keep your ears open for updates or if they call names."

∞

Dr. Prasont in a meeting with Dr. Neson states,

"Let's recap what we've done so far: x-rays of the brain and neck, MRI of the brain and neck. Look at the MRI of the brain, Dr. Neson. For both there appears to be a dark area, exactly the same dark spot. To determine the dark areas will require additional testing. Are you ready to discuss it with Mary, Raimee, and their families?"

"The sooner the better."

Afterwards Dr. Prasont agrees to attend to the families. The clock located in the waiting room shows 11:50 a.m.

Malcolm asks Byron, "Can you go with me to the workout room? I'm going to lift some weights."

Ms. Sutton goes to lunch at the on-site cafeteria. "I am in the waiting room. Can I get this lunch to go?"

Returning to the waiting room and placing her food on one of the tables, she asks the attendant located at the desk, "Have they called for the names Sutton or Alexander?"

"Not yet."

Malcolm and Byron return to the waiting room around 12:20 p.m.

Five minutes after Ms. Sutton finishes her lunch Dr. Prasont enters the room. "Are you the families of Mary Sutton and Raimee Alexander?

"X-rays and MRIs taken of their neck and brain show something. We will discuss it as soon as the ladies get here."

Mary and Raimee in wheelchairs enter the waiting area.

"The tests show a dark spot appearing in the same part of the brain for both. Our staff has planned to continue with additional testing to determine the dark spots. Additional testing will commence day after tomorrow. Dr. Neson and I, along with Dr. Gannt will collaborate for both ladies."

In a singing voice Mary asks, "What will we do for tomorrow?"

Dr. Prasont quickly responds, "No testing tomorrow; spend time with your families. All we ask is both patients stay on hospital grounds. How does this sound?"

"Wonderful," Mary replies with the biggest smile on her face.

Raimee agrees, "We will have all day. There is a swimming pool and work out room. Are we able to participate?"

"It's fine for all of you to swim and work out."

Dr. Neson calls their attention with concern. "Don't overdo it."

"Oh Lord Doc, will the dark areas require surgery?" Ms. Sutton frantically asks.

Dr. Neson explains for clarity, "The next set of tests to be performed are non invasive, no cutting. The use of a different type of machine is required. This machine is stronger than X-rays and MRI's."

"Why didn't you use the stronger machine first?" Byron asks.

"That is a good question son. I will give you the truth. This machine is very powerful. It emits seriously strong waves that we do not subject a patient to unless it is necessary. In this instance, the patients require it."

"What is the machine called?"

"I have an answer for you," Dr. Neson responds. "The name is MBI (Magnified Brain and Body Image). Dr. Prasont and I will get the both of you scheduled for additional testing. Everything we need for the two of you including all necessary machines are in this area dedicated to working with you both. In addition, several suites are included as dedicated space. Our goal is to try a different test/procedure and to keep you updated every step of the way."

∞

Attendants take both patients back to their rooms. The families can now visit.

After about forty-five minutes, Byron asks, "Mom, would you like to take a walk around the hospital grounds?"

Ms. Sutton asks Mary also.

"Okay son, it will give us something to do and get me out of this room."

They slip their housecoats on.

Byron wheels his mom out the room past the nurse's station.

Malcolm wheels his sister to the elevator.

"I want to go outside," Mary asks.

The elevator door opens on the first floor. Loads of people are ready to step in.

∞

Raimee sees a sign at the automatic doors saying Crosswalk to North wing.

"Before we finish our walk we should explore the Crosswalk and where it ends."

They all stroll up the crosswalk.

Mary tells them, "Look ya'll it leads to the Research Labs and to the Restricted Quarantine area. Hurry, let's go back to the other side."

"I'm with you," Malcolm quickly says.

BYE CANADA BYE

Mary and Raimee wait for results of the last tests performed. "What if they don't find out the problem with us Raimee?" "Let us try to keep positive and hope for the best. Have you been praying?"

"Yes I have."

Raimee continues, "Keep on and keep the faith."

Their nurses take blood pressure readings and inform them the additional testing is complete.

"Your doctors will explain any findings, and they will discuss if further testing is necessary. In addition, here are your lunch trays. Dr. Neson and Dr. Prasont should be here by 2:00 p.m."

"Thanks," Mary says.

"Thank you," Raimee follows.

Dr. Prasont and Dr. Neson enter the room at 1:55 p.m. Dr. Prasont clears his throat to capture their attention. Mary immediately turns over. Raimee does not respond. The sound of light snoring tunes the room.

"Raimee," Mary softly yells. "Wake up, the doctors are here."

"Hi doctors. Our nurses said you would be here to see us."

"Yes, we have a little information to pass on to you. I am going to have a seat. Join me Doctor Neson?"

"Test results reveal a foreign presence inside your body. This is all we know so far."

"Wait Doc; what is foreign inside me? Doctor Neson, I don't understand what you mean."

Dr. Prasont explains, "Like we said ladies, we don't know anything else. Additional testing and research is required. The tests continue to reveal that each time we find something it is shown the same in both of you."

"Oh my GOD! What is it? Why us?" Mary questions, as a tear forms in her right eye.

"I want to discuss this in more detail with you and Raimee before we discuss what your tests reveal to your families."

"Okay Doc, go ahead, please spill it. We need to know don't we Mary," Raimee encourages.

"Just as I said a little while ago, the results show a presence inside your body. I know it sounds short and blunt, but at this point it is the extent of our knowledge."

"What type of presence?" she continues.

Dr. Neson explains, "The first test revealed a dark spot, the second test a mass, and now a foreign presence. As you can see, the type of presence is still unknown. There is more to this than originally anticipated.

"We do not understand yet how it affects you physically, mentally, both or a combination of physical, mental, and other. We need to address the issues further and discuss with your families."

Dr. Prasont politely continues to explain, "What is it exactly? Is it something removable? We do not know.

"These are questions that we have no answers yet, more testing needs performed. There are too many blanks. Both Dr. Neson and I, along with other healthcare professionals including behavioral health need to get involved. A comprehensive personal plan needs to be created and implemented."

∞

Next day Dr. Gannt informs Raimee, Mary, Ms. Sutton, Byron, and Malcolm, "Both of you ladies have been discharged and given the okay to return home."

"Additional testing will begin again in approximately two months. Our office will arrange everything again. Neither family will have to pay any of the medical, lodging, food, or travel costs. Just give us time to get it squared away and get a definitive date scheduled."

"Dr. Gannt," Raimee states, "Mary and I want to thank you, Dr. Neson, Dr. Prasont, and the staff, plus the part of the hospital allowing us to be here for free. Thank you so very much."

Ms. Sutton expresses joy, as tears roll down her face, "GOD will bless your organization for the travel, research, lodging, and food given freely for the patient's family members. It is a true labor of love."

The good news has spread. Raimee and Mary have changed from hospital wear to street attire. Everyone is standing in front of the hospital door waiting to load the shuttle. Five minutes later, the Alexanders and Suttons travel to make their flight.

∞

The shuttle bus arrives at the airport one hour, ten minutes prior to departure. All luggages have checked with fifty minutes to spare. The only thing left is to go through the checkpoint.

Ms. Sutton, sort of flustered, asks, "Will fifty minutes give us enough time to grab a bite to eat, use the restroom, and get through checkpoint? What do you think?"

"I think so," Raimee answers. "We should be able to if we don't waste time, if we all get food at the same fast food restaurant, and if we eat on the go."

"Let's go for it," Byron encourages with assertiveness.

The group uses the restroom and gets something to eat with twenty minutes to spare. Fifteen minutes later, their announced flight is boarding.

∞

The Pilot announces the plane lands in fifteen minutes.

"I know Sasha and Lakeeda will want to know the outcome of our testing. Get your phone and we'll call them at the same time," Raimee suggests.

After landing, Sasha and Lakeeda receive a three-way call.

Raimee on speakerphone explains, "We're back from testing and want to share what we learned with the both of you. You two mean so much to the both of us, and keeping you in the loop is a necessity. You both are like family. The doctors could not determine exactly what the problem is with either of us. It is still a mystery and the weirdest mystery. What are the odds that two people have the same symptoms, the same testing, and end up with the same results?

"The diagnosis has gone from a dark spot to a mass, and now a foreign presence. I am serious; I hope we go for another round of testing as soon as possible. It is beginning to scare me. I like to know what's going on inside my body and I'm sure Mary does."

"I do; I want to know now."

"Guess what, the same exact diagnosis and symptoms are showing up on the tests for both Raimee and me. Now the doctors want to determine what type of foreign presence is in our bodies."

∞

Lakeeda interrupts, "Sasha, it's time to reveal ourselves and the truth."

"I agree; the time is now. Let us do it since they are back from testing at the Israel Medical Center in Canada. We need to do it before they go for their next round of testing."

"Lakeeda," Raimee emphasizes. "WHAT is going on; what do you need to reveal to us?"

"We'll call you tomorrow to discuss things. Go to bed and get some sleep. Do not worry; wait until you hear from us. Okay?"

REVELATIONS

The next day Sasha and Lakeeda call Mary and Raimee asking, "Can both of you meet us at the river underpass between Kiwana and Elbos at 7:00 p.m.? It's important."

"Sure we can, but what's going on?" Mary asks as she looks at Raimee.

"Just meet us tomorrow and we'll give you the scoop."

"Okay, can we meet for dinner? I'm always hungry after work."

"That will work, I am hungry right now." Sasha replies.

At home that evening Raimee calls Mary on the phone, "I wonder what's going on now. It sounds extremely important, don't you agree?"

"Raimee you are impatient."

"I know. I always want to know things right away."

"Take a sleeping pill and try to get some sleep," Mary suggests.

"Do you have any or should I get one of mine?"

∞

The next day when they meet, Mary asks, "What's the big rush?"

Lakeeda does not waste any time answering, "Mary, do you want to go to dinner? Let us go, sit, and talk, the four of us while we eat. You may want to be sitting when you hear what we have to tell you. Any idea of where you want to eat tonight?"

"I want Mexican."

"What about you Raimee?"

"That is good. I'm ready to eat and find out the big secret."

Everybody loads into Lakeeda's car; she heads for Menos Mexican Restaurant.

The parking lot is full. Lakeeda manages to find a spot. Good thing her car is compact. It fits in almost any available space.

The women walk into the lobby of Menos. It is as crowded on the inside as the parking lot.

"Shall we wait or leave ladies?" Lakeeda inquires for opinions.

"Stay," Mary answers.

"I don't mind waiting," Sasha replies.

"Me either," Raimee responds.

"Table for four please," Mary informs the host.

"It will be approximately a twenty to thirty minute wait," the host, informs the group.

"Okay."

Quietly, all four women sit waiting to hear their group name. Neither of the women talks within the group.

Ten minutes later the host calls, "Sutton your table is ready."

Sasha, Lakeeda, Mary, and Raimee quickly stand and taken to a booth half way toward the back.

"Okay," Raimee impatiently admits. "I can't wait any longer, get with it. Tell us what's going on; don't wait on the food."

"Yes Raimee, just as soon we place the order. I don't want the server to interrupt us too soon," Lakeeda replies.

A server places four glasses of water on the table while the main server takes orders.

After the order is placed, Sasha facing Mary while reaching out to hold her hand, professes, "My name is Friend."

Lakeeda turns toward Raimee and reveals, "My name is Acazia."

Mary responds, "I know Sasha you are a really good friend and so is Lakeeda. Raimee feels the same way about you both. What would we do if it were not for both of your friendships? It shows us how wrong it is to put everyone in the same category. Thank GOD!"

"Wait a minute. Did you just say your names are Friend and Acazia?"

Mary and Raimee turn to look at each other and immediately ask questions, stumbling over words as both throw out questions at the same time.

Raimee continues, "Lakeeda, I mean Acazia, why do you have different names? Are you undercover, FBI, spies? Are you a part of something undercover? All this time we have been around the two of you, you have been in our homes, I have taken you to visit my family, and you are not who you say you are. Are you in witness protection? People assume new identities while under protection.

"Why lie to us?"

"Please give us a chance. This is the reason we are coming clean now. Let us explain and try to get both of you to understand. Keep an open mind and heart."

Raimee cries, and with a hurtful and painful look on her face she expresses, "I had given up on trusting anyone other than GOD, myself, and Byron. The two of you come along and although it has been extremely difficult, I allowed myself to place trust in you both. Now I truly can't trust anybody."

"Yeah Sasha, or who did you say?" Mary chimes in.

Mary starts lightly stomping her foot, "My mother will be mad at you Sasha; she really likes you. Malcolm and Bobby like you also."

"Hold up; give us a chance to explain. I believe when you hear what we have to say you will understand."

"Believe you. You've been lying to us all this time, and now you say believe you."

Raimee philosophies, "Everything has been going smoothly. The friendship was just too good. You know what they say, be wary of things that are too good."

"I know I can speak for both of us. The last thing we want is to hurt either of you."

I hope that is true Friend (my Sasha) and Acazia (Lakeeda)," Mary states as she embraces Acazia, Friend, and Raimee.

"Go ahead, we're listening for now." Raimee motions with a green light to continue.

"Please, we love you. My name IS Friend," Sasha reveals.

"My name IS Acazia," Lakeeda admits.

"So, you have two names; why do you have two names? How does it affect us?" Raimee asks. "Why did you wait so long to tell us?"

Acazia tries to explain, "We have given names for our realm. When a Zenithian has finished all required trainings and is selected to go to Earth a more appropriate name is assigned for better assimilation."

Mary says in a heartfelt inside voice, "Friend, that name fits because I feel you are my friend."

Neither Mary nor Raimee respond with questions or comments to Acazia's explanation.

"Mary, you are on point and I am truly your friend."

"Acazia and Friend, I love you–no matter what your names are. I believe you; I want to hear all your explanations."

"Raimee," Acazia professes. "I'm your friend. We love you both and would never do anything to hurt you or jeopardize your lives."

"Thanks," Raimee returns. "We love the both of you; I'm sure you don't doubt that. I am keeping my mind open for a little while. Now that the initial shock of you telling us your second name has sunk in; the ability to listen for understanding is possible."

"Here goes. We are not from here; we're from another planet, a different realm than here."

"Wow! The look on both your faces is priceless. I want to say yes, there are life forms outside of Earth. In actuality there are quite a large number of non Earth beings."

"If you're not from Earth, where are you from?" Mary asks. "You look like us. If you are not from here are you an alien? Aliens have big heads and skinny bodies."

"We are from another place called Zenith," Friend responds with a tone of pride. "The inhabitants are referred to as Zenithians. It is comparable to your planet known as Earth and you are called Earthlings."

"Who else knows of you?" Raimee asks. "Is this an experiment of some sort?"

"Nobody else knows who we truly are, nobody on Earth (Earthlings)," Acazia responds as she emphasizes Earth.

"Are there others like you?"

"Yes, there are many whose purpose in life is the same as our purpose for the both of you. There is a whole realm called Zenithians. There are other Zenithians who support us here on Earth. You will have the opportunity to meet all the Zenithians responsible for the survival, teaching, and understanding for both you and Mary."

"What about other Earthlings like us, why now and why us? What is your purpose for us?"

"You will receive a detailed explanation. Right now, we need the two of you for the next week to absorb and process all the new information given you. Keep yourself and your mind open and believe."

"Now is the time for us to reveal our true identities and intentions."

Lakeeda shows herself as Acazia, Princess of Wisdom. Her dull plain face turns into a masterpiece of color. Without hesitation, Acazia whisks Raimee out of the car.

Sasha exposes herself as Friend, Princess of Peace. She whisks Mary from the car.

"You've been going through all this testing at several facilities and each time the doctors and researchers have no true answers. They have no idea and do not know what they are looking at or what to look for. Eventually something will be found out; so Friend and I want the two of you to know everything there is to know first," Acazia presents. "It's best you hear what's going on from us so you will understand."

"Can we meet again and we'll explain the rest to you?" Friend asks softly. "I'll call you tomorrow to set up a time and place to meet."

"Before we go home," Mary requests, "Please answer a question. Why do you look normal? You look just like us. Your actions, speech, and daily life are normal just like ours."

Friend shakes her finger in response, "I know what you're getting at. Portrayal of beings from other planets is the look of the typical alien–green with a skinny body and a big head. I will tell you we can look like that. We can look whatever way we choose. Most times, we choose to assimilate and blend in. Therefore, for Earth we choose looks, clothes, and hairstyles that are prevalent. We select popular hair styles and transfer to our bodies."

"Wait for us to pick you up tomorrow. We will go in just one car. Friend and I will pick Mary up first and then you, Raimee."

∞

Next evening Acazia, Friend, Mary, and Raimee go to their usual meeting place.

Friend starts the conversation, "It's time for us to return to our home. We have been gone for quite some time and our GOD and all the Zenithians are waiting for us. We must provide a status report and verbal documentation. This was a special trip taken to Earth. During our previous meeting with you, we discussed who we are. We need to discuss our reasons for coming here."

"We were sent to Earth in the form of Earthlings by our GOD to help the people that society doesn't understand; the people society basically looks down on; the people who are considered the lower crust; the people who nobody really knows, or even cares to know."

"As for you two," Acazia explains, "You don't need therapy sessions and pills; you need something else. You need a purpose, something totally different. You need us. We have with watchful eyes experienced the superiority complexes that plague the many people you deal with. Now that we have done that and the both of you have been initially informed, our assignment is complete. It is time to report back. Different assignments will be given when Friend and I return to Zenith."

Mary asks, "So you're telling me that Raimee and I are that important?"

"You are that important. Is it hard to believe?"

"Yes, I'm nobody," Mary declares with a solemn face. "Nobody ever treats me with respect. I live in a neighborhood with lots of churches and churchgoers who live on all sides of me. The ridicule and inferior treatment plagues me. I am trying to understand the reason you and Friend are here. I will try to continue to trust you with all my heart.

"Please do not hurt us. In this day and time of so much freedom it is truly hard to find a being to trust."

"The proof of something else going on is in the pudding," expresses Friend. "The proof being, the burden is on us to prove to both of you we are who we say. We mean all that we send out, and eventually you will understand we are worthy of your trust. I want the both of you to think hard about the experiences you have had in the last year. We'll discuss it in a couple of days."

Mary questions, "Just so I understand clearly you want us to think of all our experiences (personal and work)?"

"Yes you are correct. Think about and if helpful write down all the good as well as all the bad things that have happened to you. Also, think about all the good and bad you have done. Try to think long and hard."

"Now think about this," Acazia proposes. "Would you like to join us on our return to Zenith? The experience will be too great to pass on. In the next week Friend and I will leave Earth to return home."

Mary and Raimee glance at each other in amazement. "Did I hear correctly?" Raimee inquires.

"Let's see if we both heard the same thing." Mary paraphrases, "Are we asked to join our two friends on a trip away from Earth?"

"First of all," Raimee asserts, "You two share with us some weird and hard to believe story about where you're from and why you're here. Now to top it off, you ask if we want to join you on an outer space trip. If I did not know for a fact I am not sleeping I would think I am dreaming. Let me check again.

She pinches the skin on her arm. "Ouch, that hurt. I guess I'm not asleep."

Mary does not hesitate to reply, "I would love to go. How many will go with us?"

"When we leave it will be the four of us, You, Raimee, Acazia, and me."

Raimee continues, "It sounds intriguing. What should we expect? It would be nice to get away from here and all the negativity."

"Yeah, I would like to get away from the bad people talking stuff all the time. How long will we be gone? I don't want to be gone from home too long unless I can bring my family along," Mary affirms. "Family means so much to me. For a long time we have only had each other, my mom, my two younger brothers, and me. We have each other's back. To me that is a good thing."

"Mary, do not let others give you advice. Family looking out for each other is the backbone of many cultures. In African cultures, extended families are normal. It has changed from that in some societies of today."

Raimee's eyes twinkle as she asserts, "I don't care how long we'll be away. I am tired of my job. It will probably be gone when I return. A new environment and scenery might be good for my soul."

Mary claims, "I'll have to tell my mom and see what she permits. She will probably be scared for me and want to come and bring both my brothers. I'm smiling but it's true."

Acazia speaks up, "The Zenithians are expecting the both of you to return with us. This is a matter of the utmost importance to our way of life. No negative answers will be accepted for this trip."

Raimee voices, "Is it a request, asking Mary and I if we want to go? That is what you both portray."

Acazia continues with a smile as she places her hand on Raimee's shoulder, "Consider it a required request."

"Where are we going?" Mary inquisitively questions.

Raimee eagerly replies, "To Zenith, of course."

Shrugging her shoulders Mary continues, "How will we get there, will spaceships come for us?" The expression on her face depicts the sincerity of her question. Seriously, she means what she is asking.

Raimee quickly and assuredly answers, "No girl, there are no spaceships." She glances at Acazia, chuckles, and asks, "Are there?"

"We do have transportation vessels located on Zenith that are used to travel when certain needs dictate."

Friend continues describing, "You, shall I say, the four of us will travel to Zenith through Heavus. Heavus is the means of travel Zenithians like Acazia and I use."

"Heaven," Mary paraphrases, with a questionable look on her face.

"No, not Heaven, its Heavus."

"What is Heavus? It sounds like Heaven. I bet it is a place of love like Heaven."

Friend says, "Let me try to explain better Mary. Have you seen the rainbow that is in the sky after it rains? A beautiful rainbow; it's a mystery."

"Yes, I have seen them before. It's been a while, though, rainbows don't come out as often."

Raimee agrees, "Mary you are right; I haven't seen a rainbow in a long time. Why is that Acazia? I used to see them more often as I was growing up. A rainbow is a sign that GOD will not destroy the Earth by water again."

"Yes, if you have a religious, Christian belief; I think I've heard it will be destroyed by fire next time."

Mary acknowledges, "A rainbow is so beautiful. Is that the reason its name, Heavus, is similar to Heaven?"

"What does a rainbow have to do with us going to Heavus, or where you're from?" Raimee questions.

Acazia does not waste time. She affirms, "The rainbow is Heavus. It's our transportation to and from various planets, worlds, and realms."

She raises both hands, palms up, and starts to mumble.

Friend accompanies Acazia; she raises her hands, palms up.

Appearing surprised, Raimee says, "It sounds like Acazia is asking for a wish."

Instead of Friend also mumbling, it appears she agrees with Acazia by asserting approval.

After about five minutes, the mumbling ceases. Light reflections begin to show. Initially the light appears off white and changes to a darker color. The sky covered, as a rainbow appears.

"This is Heavus and it will take us all to Zenith," Acazia explains.

"It's fantastic and so pretty," Mary describes as she jumps up and down. "It's so beautiful."

Less than two minutes later, the rainbow disappears as quickly as it appears. Nothing in the sky shows a rainbow exists.

"Am I dreaming?" Raimee asks. "Smack me to wake up. Did I or did I not just witness a rainbow invoked by a chant?"

"We are traveling to and from Zenith using the Heavus," Mary confirms.

"How long in miles and minutes does it take to travel from Earth to Zenith using Heavus? Are there multiple Heavus' or just one? Do all Heavus' have the same color, design, and size?"

"Wow," Mary blurted! "That's a lot of questions Raimee."

"Sounds like fun. What about taking family?" she continues.

"Yeah," Mary quickly chimes in, "I want to take my family with me; I don't want to leave them here while I'm on Zenith. We are a close family and there are no secrets between us."

Raimee continues, "What is it like on Zenith, are the people nice; are they considered people, human beings, or what? Are they like the two of you in appearance?"

Friend replies, "They are a form of life. I will let you see that for yourselves when we get there. Life on Zenith is different from Earth, but in a good way. You will see. Once we get back, you can tell me what you think about it, how it looks, and what the people are like. You will find out soon, because we'll be leaving in two days."

Mary leans over and mumbles to Raimee, "Two days, I thought we would have at least a couple of weeks. My family doesn't know yet."

Raimee speaks to Acazia and Friend, posing an alternative, "What about our jobs? Two days does not give much time to prepare to be away. Can the return date be extended, so I can put in a two-week notice?"

"Remember previously it was stated a requirement to go," Friend reminds them. "Okay ladies go home and we'll talk again tomorrow."

"What about our families?" Mary asks again quickly.

"Sorry for the short notice and the family/work life inconvenience. No families allowed on this trip. It will be the four of us and some Zenithians that have been living on Earth helping us. Hopefully, your loving families will understand."

Raimee expresses with a question, "There's more of you here, right now? Who are they and do I know any of them?"

"Yes, there are more than Friend and myself. They have been working in the shadows. I do not think you have met any of them. Their roles are not to interact with you directly. I may have introduced one or more of them filling an intern role. In actuality they are supporting Friend and me in helping you."

"There is a movie about aliens living on Earth; you cannot tell they are aliens unless you have the special glasses that allow you to see their true form. It's true, not just making believe," Raimee continues with a slight snicker.

"People are not going to believe this; aliens live here on Earth. Aliens that look like people who communicate and act just like us. I wish my parents were alive to see this. Since they are not I am going to tell my son. He will be shocked and probably won't believe me."

"A lot of people will think I'm crazy when I tell the story of aliens," Mary insists.

"Please keep this a secret; at least for now. It is too soon to let other people know about this; and too soon to let them know about us, and why we are here. There's a lot more we need to do with the two of you, therefore, keeping this hush for now is very important."

"I can do that," Mary admits.

"I can too," Raimee agrees. "We must tell our families because we are leaving for Zenith in two days."

"Yes you are correct," Acazia explains. "Your families also must understand this should be kept strictly hush.

"Let us talk about it some more before tomorrow. We want you to understand, accept, and be willing to accompany us back to Zenith."

"Before tomorrow?" Mary asks with a questionable facial expression.

Acazia continues, "I'm talking about a phone call tonight; we don't have to meet in person. Will a three-way call suffice? Friend and I will call both of you. Does eight o'clock work for everyone?"

∞

"Do you have additional questions for us? You both asked some good questions."

"The safety of the trip and welcoming of the Zenithian people concerns me," Raimee informs Acazia and Friend.

"There is trust among the four of us?" Acazia asks Raimee, Mary, and Friend. "Am I correct?"

"Yes," Raimee assures them.

"Hold to that trust you have for Friend and me. And with that, you will know the rest is in the best of care. Again, please don't worry," Acazia says. "I won't let anything happen to you."

MARY'S REVEAL

L ater in the evening, Mary walks in the house with a big cheesy smile on her face.
Immediately Malcolm starts with questions, "What's going on; what are you so happy about big Sis?"

Mary grabs the broom, swirls an area of the kitchen for dirt, debris, and food. She does a brief dance, slightly jumps up and down, and responds gleefully, "Guess where I'm going?"

Malcolm in singsong asks, "Mary, Mary quite contrary, where do you plan to go?"

"Will you give your sister a break with the singing interrogation?"

"I'm just playing with her. She knows I love her with all my heart."

"It must be somewhere fantastic. I have not seen you this excited in quite some time. To tell the truth you never show this kind of excitement. I like it.

"Where are you going daughter?"

"In two days Raimee and I are going with Acazia and Friend to their home."

"Who?" Ms. Sutton questions with a puzzling look on her face. "Cada who and Friend, did you say?"

"I trust your friends that you have already introduced. I trust Raimee, Sasha, and Lakeeda. Why are you not spending time with them? Now you're talking about going away with people we have never met."

"Mom they are okay people, good people, and good to me."

"Where will you be going?" Ms. Sutton questions in a softer voice.

"We're going to their home, Zenith; where Acazia and Friend are from."

Malcolm jokingly asks as his eyes veer up toward the ceiling, "Is it a foreign planet? It sounds like a cartoon planet." He's laughing, "Zenith."

"Yeah, that's correct. You laugh but I think Zenith is a good name. It fits the planet. According to Friend and Acazia, the Zenithians are proud of it. It is away from here, and to me that is a good thing, so I do not care where it is. I am just going somewhere else. I will not be alone. I'll have three good friends with me."

"What way do you travel?" Malcolm questions with a smirk.

"Lakeeda and Sasha asked me not to discuss the specifics with anyone yet, not even family. I'm sorry."

"We won't tell anybody, will we mom and Bobby?"

"I cannot talk to you; I have said too much already. Keep everything I have said quiet. Okay? I will update you with everything when the time is right. I hope they do not find out that I've said anything to you. I'm just so used to sharing everything with the family. It's hard to keep you in the dark. I am not lying to you all; I just cannot tell you what's going on. I'm kinda keeping things from you. In due time I will be able to explain everything.

"Please give me a break; try to understand, and try to support me."

"Wait a minute," Ms. Sutton requests. The wheels in her brain are turning. "Did you say the names of four different people? I know I heard Lakeeda, Sasha, Cada somebody, and Friend. That is four plus Raimee and yourself, making it six people instead of four. Which of these are the right names?"

"Yes, I did call out four names. The thing is two people have two names. Acazia is Lakeeda and Friend is Sasha."

"Mom, as I said, I have actually given you more information about the trip than I should have. I'll tell you all more when I can. Just give it some time. Please trust me on this. I love you all."

"We are your family. We are a special family–no secrets. When have we kept secrets from each other?"

"Yeah big sis, we never hide anything, so let us not start now. You know our lips are sealed."

"All three of us know how to keep our business to ourselves." Bobby continues, "We are like Vegas. What goes on in our house stays in our house."

"Since I have already said them, I will give them to you again. They have Earthly names when here but also have real names used by the people of Zenith. You know Friend to be Sasha and Acazia to be Lakeeda. Now I'm gonna quit talking about it."

"Can I go with you? Ask your friends if you can take any family members?" Malcolm proposes with his hands in a prayer like position. "Please."

"I've already asked that question. I asked it as a first question. I thought of you all immediately. Going to a foreign planet is not something I want to do or somewhere I want to be without my family. Even if I would rather be there than here, I always want to be with you all. You mean everything to me.

"Family, do not think that I have or will ever leave or forget you. This is just an opportunity for Raimee and me. She loves her son just as much as I love you all. Neither of us would do anything to jeopardize that. So do not question our motives. Please, please trust me."

Ms. Sutton with motherly concern, requests, "Be sure you call me at least every other day."

"I'm not sure about that mom. I have no idea how things work there. I don't know all the communication ways that are available."

Ms. Sutton eyes Malcolm and Mary, stretching her arms to each of them.

Mary comes in for a hug, then Malcolm. Both hug her at the same time.

By now, Mary is deeply thinking. She definitely has no poker face. Heading toward the stairs she softly replies, "I'm going to bed, and don't worry mom everything will be okay."

"I love you all."

Calling it a night, she climbs into bed.

Bobby, Malcolm, and Ms. Sutton follow to her room.

Bobby asks, "What do the people on Zenith look like?"

"I guess they look like Sasha and Lakeeda; I mean Friend and Acazia. The people, life form on Zenith look like, well they look like whatever they want to look like," Mary maintains. "This is what Lakeeda and Friend told us."

"Okay, this is getting a little freaky and weird. What is she talking about?" Malcolm questions. "I thought she was joking and playing around. Now, I don't know what she's doing."

"Mary, are you playing games or are you having some problems?"

"Mary," Ms. Sutton comments softly but with a questioning and concerning tone, "Is everything okay, sweetheart? Honey, we love you and are just concerned with what you tell us. Do not get me wrong, I am happy that you share your life events with me and your brothers. I am your mother; anything you say I am open to understanding."

THE CAFE

Raimee picks Mary up and they meet Acazia and Friend at the Cafe. The menus are already at each chair of the table.

Friend, pulling the chair out asks, "What are the scoop ladies?"

"Nothing much, doing pretty good."

Raimee follows, "I'm good, can hardly wait to hear from you."

"Would you like to order something?"

"No thank you," Mary answers. "When we leave we're going to my house for dinner. Is everyone okay with heading to my house to eat after our little meeting?

"I told my family about Acazia, Friend, and Zenith; they did not believe me at first. Then after a while, they thought I was having problems. I'm sure it's a hard pill to swallow with me talking about foreign planets and aliens, especially with me saying I'm planning to leave with the aliens."

"What kind of problems do they think you are having?" Raimee asks.

"You know the mental, or shall I say mentally unstable kind. I can't even be mad or upset. Until I have a way of proving your existence, I expect to be seen as a kook."

"We are leaving in two days, so they will have to believe you and come to grips with it. Okay," Acazia encourages.

"I know," she insists, "When I get home tonight I have to put it on thick, to get them to believe in what I tell them."

Raimee reassures Mary, "It's going to be okay, don't worry. I am willing to explain everything to your family if you like."

"You are?

"Great!

"Yes, I want you to explain; they will listen if you discuss it with them. I'm ready to go now before mom sets the table for dinner. Do you know what you are going to say? It is so weird trying to explain something like this."

"Acazia and Friend will also be there for backup."

Raimee and Mary agree to meet Acazia and Friend at a mutual rendezvous point for the trip to Zenith.

∞

Mary enters the house. She states, "Mom I've brought Raimee, Sasha and Lakeeda with me for dinner."

"Hi Ms. Sutton, how are you this evening? Hello Malcolm and Bobby, it's good to see you," Raimee acknowledges.

Sasha speaks, "Hi everybody."

"Good evening, thanks for having us," Lakeeda shares. "Actually it's good to see the three of you before the four of us leave."

"Ms. Sutton, Mary is not exaggerating or having issues. We are really going to Zenith, and we're leaving with our friends Lakeeda or Acazia and Sasha or Friend. It's weird, but it is the truth. They are good people. We trust them completely."

Ms. Sutton tries to explain, "It's still hard to believe even with your friend Raimee explaining it to us. Mary, it is not that we are hard in understanding; what you are asking us to believe is weird. As your family, because we love you unconditionally we believe you and trust you. We support your decisions."

"I support you," Malcolm expresses. "I love you always."

Bobby claims, "Sis, you know you have my support. I want you to do your thing. Whatever it is, it must be special."

Malcolm, Bobby, and Ms. Sutton at the same time wrap arms around her.

"Good, I'm glad to have all three of my family with me. We are leaving day after tomorrow, and we'll be gone for about eight months."

∞

Next morning Mary glances through her clothes and around her room. She takes a basket of clothes and loads into the washer. She runs into her mother's room.

"Mom, I have only two days until we leave; I forgot to ask what I need to bring."

"Call Raimee and ask her."

"Good idea. Thanks!"

"Hello."

"Raimee, what are we supposed to take on the trip?"

"I am not sure; I am packing a variety of different items. You should do the same."

"Okay, thanks."

"I don't know why you all are leaving in such a hurry. You let me know two days before you plan to leave. Can they wait a few more days?"

"No mom, they can't."

"That's the part I don't understand. What's the rush?"

"This is the way it is mom. Please don't be upset."

ZENITH TRIP

They meet several miles outside of their homes in a town by the name of Pace. Raimee carries one large suitcase; Mary brings two bags, a medium, and a small size. Friend and Acazia travel lightly. Both have small bags.

Friend begins the chant; quickly Heavus appears.

All four ladies walk onto Heavus.

Mary utters, "Goodbye United States."

While blowing hand kisses, Raimee follows with, "Goodbye Earth."

∞

Friend and Mary glide out of the Heavus. Acazia and Raimee follow. POOF! Heavus disappears.

"Where did it go?" wide-eyed Mary asks.

"Oh my GOD, I thought it would hurt or be uncomfortable. It is so nice."

"Let's do it again," Mary says before Raimee could finish her sentence.

Acazia and Friend are laughing, "Both of you were scared for no reason."

Exhibiting a smirk smile, Raimee responds, "No reason, I was scared of the unknown and something new."

"Raimee look, it is so beautiful here."

"Yes, it is. It's really amazing, not like the moon, or somewhere desolate."

"Why the moon?"

"Well, I have never been to any planet other than Earth; all I have seen about planets is what I learned in school and what I saw on TV. I knew it would be pretty because of Acazia and Friend. They came to Earth from another world in the hopes of providing something sweet and beautiful to Earthlings; it stands to reason that the place they hail from is also beautiful."

"Do you agree Mary? You are so beautiful yourself."

Mary blushes.

Acazia and Friend inform Mary and Raimee as they walk past a lush garden of plants boasting pastel colors, "Ladies this is where the two of you will be living while on Zenith."

"Wow Acazia", Raimee voices. "The surroundings are break-taking."

Mary walks to the entrance. "Where's the key? Can we have two, one for each of us?"

Friend eyes Mary and Raimee, "We don't have a key to give you."

"No problem, we can wait until tomorrow."

"No, what I'm saying is there are no keys to give; no keys are used on Zenith."

"None?"

"None at all."

"Why?" Raimee questions.

"We don't need keys on Zenith. Everybody respects each other and their belongings."

"That is definitely something to get used to," Raimee states. "That is the first thing I do before I get out of the car is find my keys. When I get in the house the first thing I do is to lock the door and place the keys where later I can find them. I do this any place–work, or even someone else's home. It's a habit that I have always liked."

"That is a good habit. I suggest you continue using it."

Friend continues, "It's getting to be that time, time to be in our happy abodes."

Raimee and Mary admire the setup of their living quarters.

"This is going to be home sweet home for the next eight months."

"I know Raimee, look at it. It doesn't look like anything I'm used to seeing on Earth."

∞

Mary looks on the wall; she looks behind the curtain.

"It feels stuffy. I am sweating like crazy. Is there air conditioning?"

Acazia tries to explain, "The inside is to the outside. Heating and air conditioning as used on Earth does not work here on Zenith. Zenith consists of personal temperature gauges allowing personal internal regulation."

She wonders if Raimee and Mary understand what she just told them.

"How or shall I ask when will our internal temperature regulate? I'm going from hot to cold to hot. It is miserable."

"It takes about five to ten minutes for a new body to regulate. You will feel it soon. It's been six minutes."

TERMS

The next day Friend and Acazia kick off the morning by stopping by and gathering up Mary and Raimee.

Invited in, they sit in the lounge area for a short while, waiting for Raimee and Mary to finish getting ready.

"We are going on a little walk. We're taking you to visit the most high, GOD."

"A god, I cannot wait to meet them. What is their name? Your God, what's their name?" Raimee inquires.

"Xanthus. GOD is Xanthus, the ruler of all Zenith and conquered realms."

They are full of questions, especially Mary.

She dares to fire off questions immediately. "Are you family oriented? How are kids born, formed, and grow? Who raises the kids? What if any characteristics do Zenithians have like Human Beings on Earth?"

Shy Mary does not hesitate to become informed.

Friend says with a smile, "Slow down. You will have time to ask as many questions as you want. Acazia, I, and the others will give the both of you answers."

Mary laughs, glances at Friend and Acazia, and eyes Raimee with a big smile.

While on the way to visit Xanthus, Raimee beholds something familiar. Turning her head with a wide-eyed expression she comments, "I've seen these before, yet I can't remember where; what are they? They are so small."

"They are called Cherites," Acazia reveals.

"What a cute name," Raimee expresses. "Is there a personal name?"

"Now, I know where I have seen them. I don't know what they are. I see them in my dreams; they have been visiting me for years. Wow, what role do they play?"

"One of us will sit down with the both of you and explain all the roles and responsibilities."

Friend responds, "Hopefully with all the things you hear and learn pieces of the puzzle will fall into place. Believe me there is still quite a bit to learn. Be open to everything now that you are here on Zenith. Ask any question you feel will help you better understand."

"Keep on walking with us." As they continue to walk, Friend greets several Cherites

"WOW! More Cherites," excitedly Mary exclaims. "They are like tiny angels. Do you know any of their names?"

"Yes, let me introduce them. Eden, Sarna, and Elam I'd like to introduce you to our EBOI's, Raimee, and Mary."

Eden, Sarna, and Elam begin to make noises, kind of with a slight shrill. Mary and Raimee turn toward each other with confusion on their faces. By the time they turn back around Eden, Sarna, and Elam have scurried away.

"You will learn and communicate more, even with Cherites as you spend additional time here."

"Tell us about Zenith's people, planet, and beliefs. Do Zenithians fear anything? What powers and knowledge do you possess that others may want?" Raimee asks Friend.

"Our internal structure including the people and beliefs are some of the main reasons Zenith reigns. The other is GOD Xanthus. Our structure is just that, internal. Maintaining the inner workings of Zenith is through the knowledge of a few trusted Zenithians.

"Zenithians are warriors, self-preservers, and protectors of Zenith. Early in our lives, we learn that we must always protect the peaceful way of life, choosing violence only when the preservation and protection of Zenith is threatened. As we grow up, each Zenithian receives a role assignment based on skill sets. Some learn and some are born with certain skills. Others are extremely gifted. There are different roles and many are assigned the same roles.

"Everyone and I mean everyone living on Zenith is treated with respect and equality."

Mary eyes Raimee and whispers, "I don't see any other Earthlings."

"I notice that; we will stick out for sure."

Acazia laughs and responds, "Don't worry, nothing is off here. You two are just the first. Remember I told you how special you are; you will be able to see it for yourselves."

"What are the main roles of Zenithians?"

"Good question Mary," Raimee compliments.

"I agree with Raimee; very good question and I'll talk about it briefly.

Friend and I are Special Assigned Guardian (SAG).

Other roles and primary responsibilities are:

CORDER

SEA - Special Earth Assignment

GAS - Guardian Assist Support

CHERITES - dream visitors

TOURANS (lookouts)

ZAW - Zenith Allegiant Warriors

XANTHUS - GOD

I'll go into further detail on roles and responsibilities later."

"Listen up, I am not finished. There are a few terms that you should be aware of, words used with pretty much the same meaning as Earth's language for time. Please learn them immediately because all conversations spoken with Zenithians including Friend and myself will use the words that represent time on Zenith.

- for second use quib
- for seconds use quibs
- for minute use milation
- for minutes use milations
- for hour use zenot
- for hours use zenots
- for hourly use zenox
- for day use nimi
- for days use nimis
- for daily use nimix
- for week use kero
- for weeks use keros
- for weekly use kerox
- for month use metre
- for months use metres
- for monthly use metrix
- for year use luna
- for years use lunas
- for yearly use lunar
- for decade use desa

- for decades use desas
- for century use centra
- for centuries use centras"

∞

"What's your race?"

"Let me discuss it," Acazia anxiously responds. She asks, "Why, what is race?" with a look of thought on her face. "Does race matter to you?

What about you Mary?"

"Not at all," Raimee answers. "I am just curious."

"I care only about a person," Mary remarks.

"There is no separation by race on Zenith. Race is a word Earthlings created and use," Acazia continues. "We live our daily lives for lunas knowing and understanding your history. We have studied Earth for a long time. It's astonishing how all the people of Earth separate themselves into status quos by varying degrees based on race, ethnicity, culture, religion, complexion, estate, financial well-being, age, who you know or don't know, and many other things."

Raimee adds, "And that list you gave isn't all encompassing. There is a lot more to add. It is the status quo of how lives are valued or devalued based on something an individual or group of individuals feel the need or place to initiate."

"On Zenith, we are equal beings. We have a GOD, and people are equal. Both are true. We have differences in appearance as do Earthlings have different looks. Many times on Earth people judge, classify, and value or devalue others based on looks. Everybody on Zenith receives equal and respectful treatment."

ORIENTATION

Early the next nimi Acazia requests Friend to, "Please get Mary and Raimee and bring them to the New Orientation. Inform them of the breakfast table and the need to be on time. Thank you!"

∞

"Mary do you want something to drink? I am used to drinking coffee early in the morning. I don't know what this is on the table but I'm going to brew it. If you like, I can make enough for the both of us. Let me know, so I can start it brewing."

"What is it; is it coffee or tea? What about hot chocolate?"

"I don't know. It does not say coffee or tea. It's labeled Orchu Drink." Raimee tears the corner of the packet. "It doesn't smell like coffee or tea; it definitely isn't hot chocolate. It has more of a fruity smell. Maybe it tastes fruity."

"No thanks, count me out. I think I'll wait until we go for breakfast."

"I am finished in the bathroom; you can go in. Oh wait, let me get my makeup and hair stuff. I will get my clothes out when you are finished. I don't want you to think you are sharing rooms with a dirt dobbler."

"What is a dirt dobbler?"

Raimee dresses while Mary finishes her shower. She walks out of the bathroom half dressed, picks up her belongings from the bathroom and explains, "I just use the term dirt dobbler as slang for someone who keeps a messy, dirty house. It can also relate to people keeping other things dirty all the time. I am not certain if a dirt dobbler is a real name for something."

"How does the drink taste; is it good?"

"Well, it is hot. It smells fruity but does not taste fruity. There are no sweeteners to add. This is what some people might refer to as an acquired taste; you have to be the person that likes this kind of taste. It's definitely not doing it for me."

While they finish dressing, in walks Friend informing them, "Both of you will attend ZAPP today. Finish getting ready; we will wait for you."

Friend and an unknown male sit down. "This is Meta. Meta, please meet Mary and Raimee."

"Hello and good morning."

"What's the dress code for the nimi? I'm going to wear a short sleeve top with a pair of casual pants."

"You can wear whatever you want, to a certain extent," Friend replies.

Mary puts on a pair of jeans and a halter-top. The jeans are tight and the halter-top is skimpy.

Friend butts in, "I know I said wear whatever you want but now is where a certain amount of pre-knowledge is valuable. The lives of men and women on Zenith receive respect equally. No person is allowed to show unnecessary skin and body parts."

"I can't wear a halter top. Is that what you are saying? I'm glad Raimee suggested I bring a variety of clothes."

"What is ZAPP?" Raimee questions. "The spelling is ZAPP. That's funny; on Earth there is a singing group called The ZAPP band." They laugh aloud.

Friend holds a date measurement tool, similar to a planner. "The ZAPP is held every other nimi for eight metres. This date measurement tool shows the date both of you start ZAPP training through your last scheduled date."

"Okay, you have said three words I don't understand, ZAPP, nimi, and metres," Raimee continues. "Is it a foreign language? I only speak English and I'm not perfect doing that."

Friend laughs and affirms, "Remember nimi and metres are two of the words I gave you in the time list. The list contains the equivalent Zenith to Earth terms for time measurement and calculation. Pull out your list. I am going to say what they mean again; you will need to learn and recognize them as soon as possible. You will need to recognize them from communicating with others and required to use them appropriately when communicating with others.

"Nimi is the Zenith equivalent for day. Metres is the Zenith equivalent for months.

ZAPP stands for Zenith Advanced Preparation Programming. It is to relieve all the negative programming Earth has systematically and continuously made its people endure, particularly certain populations; it prepares them, the chosen ones, Earth ready."

Mary interested to know asks, "What does Earth ready mean?"

"Once ZAPP training is complete you are evaluated to determine if the programming is successful. If it is, you will soon be ready for your return to Earth."

∞

Friend returns with Raimee and Mary to the New Orientation Session.

Acazia quickly explains, "This session will help initiate you to learn what your true purpose is. In your Earthly life, others have held you down. ZAPP will help get both of you ready to determine why and how. The goal is assisting you in finding your true potential, and removing all shackles–mental, emotional, spiritual, and physical.

"ZAPP has a specific process Chosen Ones go through and endure. It is a retraining of the mind, body, and spirit. It is seeing the world and especially yourself in a different light–a more positive view. Your perspective toward inputs, outputs, and outcomes are measured. Is the glass half full or is the glass half empty?

"After each person completes ZAPP, a comprehensive performance evaluation is used to measure achieved outcomes. The evaluation and testing must be satisfactorily completed before you can return to Earth."

Raimee is eager to know, "What are the outcomes to be measured?"

"When the time comes you will know," Friend assures her. "Let us sit and discuss what's about to occur. Be on the alert, take in as much information as possible, and try to comprehend as much as you can. Will you try to do this for yourself?"

"It is all good. We will do what makes you happy," Raimee promises.

"It's not for me but for you," Friend encourages. "Ask questions, learn, understand, and don't forget, ask questions until you understand, both of you."

"Okay," Mary agrees.

Raimee responds, "I will do it for myself."

∞

Mary and Raimee go to the front and sit during the orientation session.

Xanthus speaks first, "Let us personally welcome our newest, Mary and Raimee. This is their first few nimis on Zenith. Show them how good Zenith can be for them."

Acazia leads, "Welcome Raimee."

Friend speaks, "Welcome Mary."

The assembly follows, "Welcome Raimee, welcome Mary."

Xanthus sits and Acazia stands beside him.

"When I get the chance I'm going to ask Acazia if anything special is going on with her and Xanthus. The two of them act seriously engaged and seemingly mesmerized in each other's eyes."

"Xanthus, Zenithians, and friends, let us thrive and continue to grow. Mark this occasion for it is special indeed," Acazia hails. Everyone claps.

The clapping continues for over two milations.

Sporting a caring smile, Acazia eyes Mary and Raimee.

Mary and Raimee embrace by holding hands.

Within quibs, "ZENITH, ZENITH," the entire assembly yells. "Strength and power to all Zenith."

Mary whispers to Raimee, "These people truly have pride in their planet."

They observe as much as possible checking other facial reactions; they quickly glance at each other and back to the front of the assembly area. The room is crowded.

Mary glances around and a young man has caught her eye. Apparently, she has also caught his eye. It takes him awhile to find a seat; he takes a second, then a triple take, and gives Mary a big smile.

Everyone watches the person in front of them and to each side of them and finally to the very back of them; all begin to sit down.

∞

Without warning or a hint from the speaker, a sort of meditation starts with slight chanting.

Mary and Raimee are still there so they play along, lips slightly moving.

They eye each other and shrug their shoulders because neither of them understands the chant.

The chanting continues for some fifteen milations.

"This is my opinion," Raimee comments. "It is not a staring chant, where the group is in a trance, but friendly and welcoming. Voices are soothing instead of eerie."

The assembly is still in place; the chanting dies down and continues for five milations. After the chanting subsides, the majority of the assembly yells, "Welcome Raimee, welcome Mary."

Both ladies observe, address the assembly with a smile, and a nod silently saying, "Thank you, thank you."

"Thank you, I'm glad to be here," Raimee proclaims.

Mary agrees, "I'm also glad to be here."

Both ladies embrace, hold hands, and display a genuine interest in the proceedings.

Raimee whispers to Mary, "The chant in the assembly appears harmless, yet I'm not sure if it is prayer or what. I am not sure what they are saying. I do think it's interesting."

After about one zenot, the assembly dismisses and all Zenithians leave, going their separate ways. Raimee and Mary observe, noting everyone's reactions. Mary asks Raimee, "Do we mingle or just leave? It appears everybody is leaving. Should we do the same?"

DEBRIEF

Raimee and Mary head toward their shared living assignment, ready to call it a night.
"I'll take my shower first."
Before Raimee can finish her words and head to the bathroom, a knock is at the door. It is Friend, Acazia, and Meta (one of the other Assistant Guardians).

Friend asks politely, "May we come in for a short time to talk?"

"Yes, come in. We're taking our showers, getting ready for bed."

After entering, Meta immediately asks, "What do you think of your first assembly? Did you get anything from it? Can you share your feelings?"

Raimee responds, her tone sounds frustrated, "We are headed to bed but don't mind giving a brief response."

Mary answers first with the quickness, "It was a good event, and the memories will stay with me for a very long time. Chanting is new to me so I'm interested in how it's done."

"It was okay. We need an explanation of what the assembly is about and the chanting performed," Raimee informs them. "After listening to that for over one hour and not understanding a word or what it is about, I feel left out and lonely. I do not feel a part of the assembly. We're here to be a part of your world, correct?"

"You better believe it," Friend responds. "Everything we do will be to include you both. You will come to discover, learn, and understand all that is Zenith, all that is the Zenithian way, and all that is for you two. We have no secrets about your reason for being here and you can trust that your being here is all-good. This first assembly is to give you a glimpse at one of the things we do. It is also to introduce you to the Zenith community and allow the community to see the two of you. You both are well received.

"The chanting is a regular part of Zenithian nimix life. You will be taught how to understand what the chants represent and how to perform them along with your participation.

"It is understandable the way you are feeling. That is where we come in. We can explain what is happening and make things here a little clearer. Once we explain and you continue to be a part of Zenith, everything will be clearer; give it a little time. You will be here for eight metres. During your stay it is our hopes you become a true part of Zenith. After completion of the ZAPP training both you and Mary will better understand Zenith and better understand yourselves, your life, and the planet you come from, EARTH. You shall have a better understanding of the planet Earth and how to cope with its societal influences, mainly the planet, how they think, why they do the things they do, and most of all finding your true self."

"Thanks for participating and trusting us unconditionally." Acazia expresses. "The next two nimis we'll be showing you around, allowing you to view nimix activities and interactions. I hope that it will help you better understand and assist with transitions of how things are on Zenith. I promise you."

"People treat each other well. Have you noticed how they treat the women? What I mean is I see the men treating women well. I have noticed a little of that already. It is not because of sex or even sexual in nature, but respectful, kind, and truthful–a social blossoming. There's an outer peace on Zenith." Chuckling, Raimee voices, "Earth men can learn an awful lot; I'm not being sexist, the women can also."

∞

Meta, Friend, and Acazia bid Mary and Raimee a good night and walk away. Meta's face now has no unique features, his appearance the same as the other Zenithians. Every Zenithian appears to have the same look, almost clear and opaque at the same time. Friend and Acazia's looks remain the same. The facial appearance does not trigger an alarm.

A ZENITHIAN NIMI

The next nimi Meta walks Mary and Raimee around so they are able to view what happens on one of many Zenith nimis. At the end of nimi two, both attend a two-day debriefing. Friend, Acazia, and Meta are on the schedule to attend.

"What do you think about your first two days? Did a particular event or activity stand out or capture your interest?" Meta asks.

"Yes," Mary replies. "I notice how every person is always nice to each other, which is something else Earthlings could learn. I'm definitely not used to that."

In response, Raimee states, "A lot of things interest me; my head is reeling. The things that stick out the most are the nimix interaction among men and women, women toward other women, and men toward other men. There appears to be harmony.

"Am I correct in what I think?

"I like the way Xanthus commands a room. It appears he is very likable. He is strong with lots of energy, charisma, and understanding, among other qualities. Is this true?"

Acazia readily responds, "I would definitely say so. He has been the God for Zenith for many lunas. You will hopefully see it for yourselves."

Raimee adds, "I recall the excitement felt from the first time hearing his speech. I can't wait to be a part of Zenith's community for the next eight metres."

"I do want to know how long many lunas is? How old is Xanthus?"

EARTH DISASTERS

F our nimis later, Mary answers a knock at the door.
Meta summons, "Raimee and Mary, it's time for a community
event. Finish getting ready, and come with me to the Gather. It
is an area where a number of Zenithians meet as part of a community
affair. At this event the community share, engage, and discuss
discoveries and events, past and present.

"It has been twenty milations since I knocked and thanks for
opening the door. How long before the both of you are ready to
leave?"

"Give us five more milations," Raimee answers.

The three of them are walking; nobody is talking. It's so quiet.

Raimee interrupts the silence, "How are you doing Meta? What's on
the agenda?"

"I'm doing well; I don't know what it's about."

Meta drops the two off in the hands of Friend.

After approximately five milations of standing and waiting, Friend
requests of Mary and Raimee, "Come in and sit."

A flash of light flickers; talking is heard from other than Friend,
Mary, Acazia, and Raimee.

A finger points up to the sky. Mary asks, "What is that? Is that a
movie projection screen in the air?"

Raimee raises an eyebrow as she eyeballs Mary. "I don't see what
it's projecting on; it looks like 100 feet, maybe more of projection in
the sky. How is that possible without a screen? I have never seen that,
but I am thrilled. You know I love movies; it seems Zenith is a lot like
Earth, at least with certain things."

"There's a special field that allows us to project and see images
without a screen," Acazia informs of the functionality. "Look up again.
Night time is all that's needed."

Mary questions, "Is it a movie we will be watching? I love movies,
what's the title? Is Netflix up here?" she laughingly asks. "I don't care;
I'll watch just about any movie. I am ready, let the movie begin.
"Where's the popcorn, candy, and soda?" she continues while
laughing.

"No, it's not really a movie, but truthfully you should look at it and think about what you see," Acazia declares. "It will be extremely interesting and informative. I hope it will help to provide a learning experience."

Mary wiggles into place. "Where are the rest of the people?"

"All other Zenithians have seen it, some more than once."

∞

Before Acazia finished talking, a big explosion appeared on the invisible screen–fires burned rampantly.
- Shootings - police on black men and women
- Shootings - man on man
- Modern day Sodom and Gomorrah–too much nudity, and freedom with sexual public displays.
- Floods
- Tsunamis
- Drought - land is so dry, animals and people have no water
- Poverty
- Slavery from the time of the Egyptians enslaving Hebrews to the enslavement of Black peoples in the America's–Hebrews built statues for Egyptians; Blacks built America.
- People considered financially fit in society who have verbally degraded and undermined others who are not. "I don't want all people to have the ability to receive healthcare."
    "Those comments were made by some co-workers at a utility company where I used to work. They expressed their feelings against those less fortunate."
- Raimee was bullied as a child.
- Raimee cried her eyes out as she prayed to GOD and begged for his love and mercy.
- Raimee at the age of seventeen sadly expressed as she looks up into the heavens, "I feel like an alien; I don't belong here. I am so different from others. GOD, why did you put me here?"
- Raimee's abuse from her boyfriend. He hit her because she touched his car after an argument.
- Conniving, people who throw others under the bus, take others ideas, and pat them on the back all the time get all the kudos. Tareice and Trent take Raimee's ideas.
- The neighborhood and children harassed Mary because of her illness.
- Mary acted passively when being disrespected.
- Raimee and Mary see things and people for who they truly are. Those who treated them like crap their entire lives are extremely rotten, foolish, and sinful.

"You were shown visuals, some of world events, some of each of you personally. How did viewing those images make you feel?"

Raimee remembers and replies, "Those personal snippets are just some of the bad deeds people have done against me. It reminds me of how nice, honest, and loyal I was to the very persons not so nice, honest, and loyal to me."

"Did the snippets distress you? Did they call up old wounds?"

"Yes, it is hurtful," Mary, affirms. "It brings back unpleasant memories."

Mary cries, "I feel like I just relived some terrible times in my life. It hurt a lot."

Friend places her arm around Mary and sympathizes, "I figure it did, and I'm sorry. You will become a stronger person because of this. I promise you."

Raimee vocalizes, "Wow, how have I made it this far in my life? I have no person to assist me. The struggles I endured were real. Why did people treat me so bad? It's devastating to behold the mistreatment. It opens up wounds, and they do not feel so old. They feel fresh and cut to the bone."

SEEKING LOVE

Acazia interrupts the negative thoughts and feelings, "Tomorrow will be a better day, not so depressing. You will start another piece of your specialized training, and learn facts about people, events, and ways to adapt and cope. Why don't you clean up and get ready to eat."

∞

The following nimi Raimee and Mary make their way to the training area. More lush gardens boasting magnificent arrays of color dance against the fountains that flow, never to run over.

Barely audible, Mary hums a little tune. It is apparent her tunes have some rhythm.

Quickly entering and taking their seats Raimee asks, "What's on the agenda this nimi?"

Mary adds, "Yeah, what will you teach us? Can you give us some paper and something to write with to take notes?"

Acazia reveals, "You don't need to take notes. You will receive encouragement and eventually expectations to learn and remember the teachings in your head."

"What kind of mind games do you think they are playing on us? Taking notes is how I remember."

"I am with you Mary. Everything appears on the level. Both of us will have to learn very quickly how to go with the flow. If they say no note taking, we will have to step up our brainpower. I am sure we can do it. Until we have challenges that make us uncomfortable, our potential is not pushed. Here they will probably push us to a harder limit so we can reach more of our potential.

Raimee continues, "Don't worry, we will make it through. I believe and have faith and I want you also to have faith."

In walks a female, radiating femininity and a no-nonsense vibe who immediately introduces herself, "Hello, I'm Lorga. This nimi we have a busy schedule. Xanthus and Oris will sit in for a little time. Let us get started.

"Welcome to the training for ZAPP that will help to reinforce self-respect, self-esteem, and pride. Who do we have with us?"

Acazia motions and silently lip the words, "Announce yourselves."

Raising her hand, "My name is Raimee."

Raising her arm and flittering her fingers she says, "My name is Mary."

Lorga asks, "Who can tell me what ZAPP stands for?"

Mary raises her hand, "Zenith Advanced Preparation Programming."

"Yes, that's very good. ZAPP will equip you with a multitude of things. It will give you the ability to speak in public with grace, dignity, and tact. The goals are to also give you the tools to learn the various systems of how to influence people and to recognize the various games that people play and have always used on you and others like you.

"Tell me about yourselves. What are you thinking about right now? Who wants to go first?

Lorga's eyes hone in on Mary and next on Raimee. At first she does not look specifically, but after a few minutes and neither lady initiates the discussion, she requests, "Mary please go first."

"I don't really know; I feel I'm a good person, a loving and honest person. I am dependable and can be trusted. I see the good in me; others do not see me. Nobody treats me the way I treat him or her. I have had no person ever on my side."

∞

"Society places a lot on me. I have been enduring and overcoming many struggles. Our family is under a lot of pressure and stress, but our family sticks together for each other.

"Most times, I am not treated as an equal; I am treated as inferior. It creates introversion and shyness. I have only my son on my side. He is my friend and my rock. I do not have friends and do not care for any. My son is my Earthly friend. The many people I have let in my life and try to be their friend have all burned me in some way or another.

Raimee continues, "I hope now that I can consider Friend, Acazia, Xanthus, Meta, and the Zenithians as part of my family and I part of theirs. And as my family I will receive love and understanding; I hope that I can count on this nuclear family."

Acazia follows up, "It is our hopes that you will consider us as friends and family. Hopefully we are moving in that direction."

"It will be the first time that someone outside of my small immediate family truly has my best interest at heart and shows me the love I need."

Xanthus' empathetic response, "I know what you mean Raimee, we have a lot of things happening on Zenith now. I am a God, but I am a widowed God, widowed for eleven lunas and no offspring. Believe me, this is not what I want or is it the way things should be. A Goddess should stand with me, by my side."

"What age were you when married?" Raimee asks in a concerned sympathetic voice.

"We met, fell in love, and married when we were both young–I was twenty, she was nineteen. We were truly in love. At the age of twenty-two after a brief illness she died. I was ill prepared for her death. It was very hard for me. Now at thirty-four lunas I am ready for a wife. I will keep my sights open and my heart treasured. Not to seem arrogant, during all the time I have been a widow I guess in Earthling terms I am a good catch. Women from all the different worlds fall at my feet and long to be my companion and wife."

Mary eyes him, raising both eyebrows, "Are they beautiful?"

"Yes, their appearances are many and usually most of them are strikingly beautiful. Just think, women from everywhere wanting to be with you. I know one of the reasons is because I am Xanthus, and I am not bad looking. I do not think there is anything wrong with any woman; there is a woman for everyone. I happen to know what type of woman I need and want. I do not want just a pretty face to fill the position of Goddess, Xanthus' bride. I want someone truly special who will not only completely and utterly love me but also complete me. I am not like a lot of male species, thinking that youth and beauty is what makes a female the best choice. Believe me I will keep my eyes open and my radar to the wind. When the time is right, and more than likely it will happen, the woman for me will present herself.

"On Zenith, the women think they know what kind of woman I want and need. Just as they come in many different looks, I hope to meet a woman whose outward beauty is not the only feature going for her and not the only benefit for me.

"I need and want a particular kind of woman. A number of different women do many things to try to get to me. What they do not understand is there is only one woman I long for and it probably will not be the one Zenithians will expect. Women of other realms always try to cozy up to me, if you know what I mean.

"The women of other worlds visit Zenith to charm me using their wily ways. I am not like worldly men; I will not fall for their deception. Many of them will and do a myriad of things trying to win me but those things will not weaken my strength. I cannot allow their charms to captivate me. It is necessary I stay strong and not fall prey to feminine tricks. My choice will be for love, devotion, and strength.

"Even gods get lonely," Xanthus speaks with the strength of a true GOD and the calm of openness. Do you think because I am GOD, powerful, and have many that follow, I do not seek the love of a good woman? Most beings need love. Do you agree?

"Is love something you both seek?"

Sadly Mary admits, "Boyfriends I've had, but none have been in love with me. Yes, it would be nice to find that special one and get married."

Raimee professes, "Yes, it is something I want and need, and I have for some time. I found it once and it found me, but I have it no more. I have always heard that all good things must come to an end. Why does it have to be love?

186

"Many times my heart aches because of the love for someone who didn't carry the same torch for me. Time will only tell if love comes around again. If it does, I pray that I will recognize it. The many pains and heartaches keep me guarded."

"I shall keep my eyes open and guard my heart. The one I choose will be everything to me and I will be everything to her. We shall gain each other's love, loyalty, and earn each other's trust. The love of a good woman is so hard to come by, even more so as Xanthus. I want them to want me for the husband I can be, not the GOD they see. I want to take my time, because once you fall, love is blind. Rushing into affairs of the heart has been a problem with the peoples on many realms.

Continuing, Xanthus imparts wisdom, "Earth beings especially, we have observed, don't for the most part take the time to get to know each other. It's all about rushing the situation and getting into the physical portion of a relationship."

"I say that all the time. People do not want to go on dates without sex being a part of it. I'm sure you have researched Earth being relationships," Raimee expresses. "You are definitely different than a lot of the Earth men.

"I try to explain one reason. Many times, it is because of our women. We freely give into men. Earth men do not have to be loyal, honest, or trustworthy. As women we allow them to have us and other women at the same time just so we can say we have a man."

∞

"It's been eleven lunas since Olinas departed to the Everlong Realm. Eleven long lunas without my beloved; I am now thirty-four lunas born, with no partner and no children to share. I'm more than ready."

Xanthus walks slowly toward the adjoining balcony, "Olinas," he calmly calls out.

Mary comments, speaking before thinking, "You are the GOD and ruler of Zenith, Xanthus. You have it all, a great, mighty, powerful realm, and many loyal Zenithians depending on your wisdom and guidance to keep you busy. How can you be lonely?"

Raimee chimes in, "Mary you should watch what you say to Xanthus. He doesn't deserve to hurt."

"I'm sorry, that's not for me to say," Mary apologetically acknowledges. "It isn't meant as a bad thing or to make you feel bad. Really, I'm saying how good and together you are.

"Please forgive me."

MATCHMAKER

Several metres pass and Javenne, Xanthus' mother approaches him.

Javenne, very attractive and well kept, is fifty-five lunas born.

"Xanthus, the word around is you're seeking a wife. Is this true son?"

Raimee puts in her two cents, "Javenne reminds me of a Southern meets Northern Earth woman, not a diva. Her hair is in a kind of up do with a striking facial appearance, and her wardrobe is that of the 70's meets 80's era.

Go figure."

Xanthus speaks, "Mother we have guests in the room. Please say hello to Mary and Raimee visiting us from Earth. They are the first two EBOI's."

Her appearance is together and regal. "Hello, it's so nice to meet you both.

"Well is it son?" Javenne continues to ask. "I'm still waiting for the answer to the standing question."

"Yes Mother, I guess you can say it is true. I am ready. I didn't actually broadcast it; it was told in confidence and privacy."

Xanthus smiles and continues, "There is some kind of rumor mill no matter where you call home, Zenith or Earth."

"My dearest son, I'm with you on this, and so glad to hear it. It does my heart good to know you are ready. You need a goddess; Zenith needs a goddess. Let's organize a gathering so you can view suitables," Javenne ardently expresses. "Will you be okay with your mother setting this up specifically for you to find a match?"

"You have my blessing mother–pursue and prevail," Xanthus chuckles. "But Mother this will be my choice and I will take my time–little or as long as I need. Do you agree?"

"Okay dear, I'll think of the best way to present a varied selection for you."

"Mother you know it must be with taste and respect."

Confidently she ratifies, "I wouldn't have it any other way; only the best for one such as you.

She reveals to Mary and Raimee, "Several possible suitors have graced Xanthus with their presence. Not only is he a fair and just GOD, he is a gentleman with the opposite sex. This is probably one of the most important reasons they love him. Most Kings are demanding, cold, and standoffish. Yes, they lavish their loves while courting but just like mortal men when the fire wanes so does the loyalty for their marriage. As a God, they expect him to act like Kings. Not Xanthus, he is a true husband, loyal and dedicated to the end. Women from all over know this."

"That is so true," remarks Legara.

Javenne turns around with a smile on her face and inquires, "Legara when did you come in? Did you hear everything?"

"No I didn't hear everything, just enough to say if I were younger and in the market for a husband, I'd put my bid in," as she laughs as if she is busting a gut. Legara, a forty-nine lunas young Zenithian woman has been friends of the family for many lunas.

Three females walk by speaking aloud as if they want Raimee and Mary to hear. "There's no need to worry about those two. They are Earthlings. Xanthus will never bring an Earthling in as a goddess."

Thinking aloud Raimee agrees *they do not have to worry; Xanthus has his choice of strikingly beautiful women, to give me any thought.*

MERIDIUS

Raimee and Mary have lived seventy-four nimis on Zenith. Both go to the Planning Room. A sign outside the door flashes ZAW's only.

Mary comments to Raimee, "The sign says ZAW's, yet we are allowed to enter. What do you think?

No sooner than Mary's feet touch inside the room she proceeds with questions, "Oris what are you looking at?"

"Yeah what is that you are looking at and through?" Raimee copies. "It's a big piece of equipment that resembles a telescope, although it looks much different."

"He's been looking through the equipment for hours," Friend answers. "It's called a Kanwabe and it serves some of the same purposes as a telescope except it's more powerful and has many more benefits. A telescope allows you to view some planets and stars through a powerful telescopic lens. Earthlings use telescopes to view the Moon, other planets, and space. The Kanwabe's feature allows us to view any planet or realm with spot on precision. Some of the benefits allow visual access through any surface or material and an audio to know specific communication from where and by whom. There are many other features and benefits."

"What do you think about the Kanwabe?"

"It appears to be in a class by itself," Raimee states as she admires the Kanwabe. "Earth probably doesn't have anything like it. I have looked through telescopes before and they definitely do not have the features and benefits you just listed. Where do you get something like that? Is it made here on Zenith?"

Placing her hand on it as if petting the Kanwabe, Acazia responds, "Yes it is developed and manufactured from a natural substance found on Zenith and performs better than expected. Zenith is home to some very interesting, intellectual, intelligent, creative, and scientific minds."

"Do you think any other realm or planet has the same capability?"

"I hope not. I am sure this is one of the reasons for so many of our successes. Using some of the Kanwabe's features and benefits, Zenith is maximizing their abilities to know what our allies and most important our enemies are doing."

Before Acazia can finish, Oris interrupts yelling slowly; he is thinking before speaking. "Oh no, I see something going on, some type of activity on Meridius. From the looks, it will not be pleasant."

"Oris, what is it?" Ketos asks.

Ketos runs and looks through the Kanwabe, pressing several buttons. It makes slight movements.

"What activity?" Acazia promptly inquires.

Mary's face has a frightened look as she turns to acknowledge Raimee's expression.

"The planet Meridius is changing colors. It's gone from red to gray," Oris relays with concern.

"Nintho," Oris instructs with urgency, "Transmit to Xanthus what's happening. Also, as soon as I give you updates, you will need to forward the update to him."

Nintho cups his palm placing it around his left ear. Upon doing this his thoughts transmit to Xanthus. *"Meridius is now alternating red and gray."*

Acazia describes how thoughts transmit. "It is a special skill Nintho and other Zenithians are born with. While on Zenith Mary and Raimee, we will find out your special skills, learned or innate."

Xanthus transmits a follow-up, "Don't sound the alarm yet. Doing so, we will also alert Meridius that we know. You never want to let the enemy know what you have up your sleeve.

Hold off for a brief moment; let us see what transpires. A sneak attack strategy is possible. Keep me posted with each significant action or reaction; at least every five milations."

"I have never heard of a planet changing colors before. What does that mean?" Mary questions.

"It's known that various planets are shown as different colors; changing colors is somewhat different. Do you agree?" Raimee asks.

Focusing on the activity going on, Oris replies, "There is imminent danger; Meridius is and has always been a troubled planet. When the Meridians feel a threat or are ready to wage war the planet turns a pale dead gray; it is their way of letting others know to beware–war is imminent."

"Why are they declaring war, and who are they declaring it against?"

"Raimee, I will assume any planet they don't get along with," Xanthus answers, as he calmly enters the room. "Currently it is probably against Zenith."

"You are a peaceful planet," Raimee continues. "What happened between Zenith and Meridius for this unfortunate turn of events to begin? Is there anything that can be done to call a truce?"

"Meridius and Zenith have a history. The issues between us hatched many lunas ago. Meridius is not interested in peace.

Xanthus comments on his observance of Raimee and Mary, "Lots of questions, a bombardment of questions.

"It is okay; ask as many questions as needed. You should learn as much as you can about our planet. You are here for that purpose. Many times in the past Zenith and its intentions provided revelations to various planets and realms for the same reason we came to Earth. We traveled to other planets in hopes of bringing a peaceful existence by showing them a way of living as done on Zenith. The revelations to other planets were performed on a larger scale, meaning lots of inhabitants versus just the two for Earth."

"What were the outcomes?" Raimee asks.

Mary is anxious with gazing eyes, her voice slightly trembling, "Are we safe here? Will the war with Meridius be fought on Zenith?"

Noticing Mary's anxiety, Xanthus explains, "Most inhabitants on other planets are evil, extremely corrupt, and very good at mistreating their families, friends, neighbors, and co-workers. It is not only the elite, but also wealthy, rich, and even common folk. When I speak of common folk, I am referring to middle-class in wealth–those earning $100k-$250k plus. People earning six figures are just as good at mistreatment as are the rich (millionaires) and wealthy (billionaires).

"Many families are broken because of money. Family members actually kill one another for financial gain; many times, it is not for large sums. It is pretty much a common thread among other planets and realms. They are vicious to everyone they deal with, showing no real love, no loyalty. It is all about the achievement of money and power. We are not sure if they are too blind to see or care about the treatment of a majority of its citizens.

"It is in their nature. Meridius continues down that destructive path.

"If a person has lots of money, power, or influence, society as a whole treats them well. Character plays a small role in the various treatments of different individuals.

Xanthus continues his philosophy, "Hear Me, and understand. Money is not a bad thing if used properly–without greed, if equitable, and not gluttonous. However, on certain planets and realms they use the money improperly.

"The Powerful structures become overly greedy. The distribution of wealth is not equitable, and people indulge in every pleasure to the fullest and beyond. Some of the wealthy do everything possible to stay wealthy and nothing to help their less fortunate fellow man, woman, or child.

"Gluttony, overindulgence, greed, and lack of caring for its most vulnerable citizens fuel the flames of sin like lighter fluid fuels a fire. The knowledge of the minority having so very much and the majority having so very little doesn't seem to faze the minority."

"Unfortunately our efforts and many attempts are futile," Friend chimes in. "We are unsuccessful. No matter what is done to open their eyes to see what they are doing is wrong, and of no avail. The refusal of each planet or realm to provide better treatment to its people is blatant disrespect. Xanthus can't take it anymore. Plans are to destroy all planets, all realms, and all inhabitants that will not change.

"The destruction of all planets and realms is lax and not carried through. Many planets and realms remain intact. Meridius is one of the planets intact. Xanthus bides their time, giving plenty opportunities to come around. The ruler of Meridius causes mayhem and confusion on its realm and to its people.

"Mary or Raimee do you have any questions?"

Xanthus leaves the area heading toward his living arrangements, leaving Acazia, Friend, Oris, and Ketos to carry on with Raimee and Mary.

Oris steps up; he explains, "Xanthus and his most trusted advisors met several keros discussing strategies that ultimately guarantee the destruction of Meridius."

Xanthus sends a mental message to Oris and Ketos, "Meet me at the assembly room in one zenot."

For the next zenot while waiting for the meeting, Xanthus relaxes on his throne.

One zenot later on the dot, in walks Ketos and Oris announcing, "We're here, Xanthus. What are we to do?"

"Gather your fighters and prepare to attack and destroy within three nimis. I will ride with you."

"Is this attack and capture?" Ketos questions.

Xanthus does not hesitate with his response, "No, destroy all of Meridius. The number of estimated fighters will depend on the strategy chosen. A destroy mission will require less fighters."

Ketos and Oris bow and start to leave the area. While walking back Ketos suggests, "Meet me in the fighter pod area in thirty milations. We will put our plan in place."

∞

Xanthus stands up, "You both are aware of all the talks with and about Meridius. It is a wasteland of individual people making their own rules, lust, lies, deceit, violence, and destruction. It is time to make a move. The time is now; we have no time to waste.

"The day has come. For many a season we have tried everything possible to awaken Meridius to the unequal treatment of certain inhabitants. They continue to destroy themselves by destroying the lives of others. Why is it so difficult for others to see a gluttonous, power trip, and inferior thinking way of life is detrimental and not beneficial for anyone?"

ZENITHIAN ALLEGIANT WARRIORS

X anthus orders ten fight commanders to the pod room. Adamantly he admits, "This is a call to action. Meridius is now at the top of our list. They have never been an ally of Zenith or played the role of peacemaker. Many a Meridian has suffered and fallen at the hands of the Power Structure and self identified. The time has come; we are ready. We shall gather and annihilate all those on Meridius except those who accept the Zenithian philosophy, the way of life to a peaceful co-existence.

"The following fight commanders step forward: Vonth, Codus, Niese, Morik, Hahn, Ikee, Oris, Locephus, Prag, and Jarup." All ten men step forward looking straight ahead.

"I charge each of you to put together your best army of ten and prepare to attack in four nimis. Ikee, Prag, Vonth, and Jarup you shall lead. Morik, Hahn, and Codus pull the middle and Oris, Locephus, and Niese will bring up the rear.

"Do you have any questions? Please let me know now.

Xanthus waits about fifteen quibs, "Oris, I charge you with leading the entire troop to Meridius."

Oris nods his head forward and down showing appreciation and agreement with Xanthus' request.

"Wait Prag," Xanthus calls out. "I'm placing you in charge of locating bodies from Meridius that want to leave and follow us to Zenith. You know the drill; report back to me within three nimis."

Prag happily answers, "Thanks Xanthus. It will take some time to get through all of Meridius."

"I understand. You will have five of your warriors and it will be helpful if the other commanders commit their teams. Who will assist Prag with locating willing Meridians that want to accompany us back to Zenith before the attack? Each commander will lead their team and report to Prag."

"Do either of you have any comments or questions regarding the attack? If you have requests please direct them to Oris."

Raising one finger, Hahn expresses, "I have concerns about the complete and utter destruction of Meridius. Are we sure this is a decision that must be made?"

Xanthus defends his rationale, "The quest for Meridius to understand the roles that must be played is absolute. There are many times I and other Zenithians have tried to tactfully communicate and discuss how Meridius will fit into the total overall current and future plans including the roles and responsibilities for certain Meridians."

Oris asks, "GOD Xanthus, the number of soldiers preparing for battle attack is a smaller count than usual? Normally our attack numbers are 250 or more."

"Yes Oris, there is a decrease; the number of soldiers needed is 111. It should ensure our victory and their defeat.

Xanthus continues, "If all goes to plan there will not be a need to land on Meridius until the air strike is complete. The strategic plan is to air strike. As you well know, an air strike can significantly limit the number of casualties to our own warriors. It also depends on what the goals are that we want to reach. If we enter into a fight to conquer then a land attack is necessary. If our goal is to destroy the planet, its inhabitants, and every living thing upon it, then the air strike approach is best. After the air strike the 111 member troop will land on Meridius to ensure total destruction is complete."

"I understand and honor your request at once," is Oris' steadfast reply as he heads toward the fighter ships.

Prag, Oris, and Ketos enter the fighter troop bay.

Prag requests, "I need five men to accompany each of the fight commanders to Meridius in search of living bodies wanting to leave for Zenith. Step forward to show a willingness to participate."
Several soldiers step forward.

"Thanks men. All ten-fighter pods will go. At first light on the third nimi, Meridians who choose will be brought back to Zenith."

∞

It is nimi light; two ships are cast, two additional, two more, and two more, then the last two make their way toward Meridius.

The ships land on the part of Meridius pre-determined to be outside of the scope of Meridius' detection. It is a section of uninhabited land.

∞

The third nimi scouring Meridius by foot, sixty soldiers were able to meet the deadline for finding those Meridians interested in converting to the Zenith way of thinking and living.

Meridius' estimated population is 45,000. Between all sixty soldiers, 1,700 Meridians transported and now safe on Zenith.

According to Prag, "Of the remaining 43,300, a large majority stated they would have to think about it; others say maybe they would leave in three to four keros."

∞

Returning to Zenith, Prag, Oris, and Codus meet with Xanthus to discuss their findings.

Xanthus' leadership shines. He remarks, "We welcome with open arms the 1,700 returning with you. As for the remaining 43,300 beings, we cannot worry about. They too have been spoken to on numerous occasions, this being the last, and final."

Oris, Codus, and Prag share and finalize strategies for 'D' Day (Destruction Day). After meeting approximately four hours, Oris calls for a meeting with the other seven fight commanders to finalize details.

Codus informs Xanthus, "All fight commanders and their troops are prepared."

Oris speaks, "Troops it's time to keep the peace. Make sure all perimeters are contained. Right before nimi light, we will launch an attack. Ten fighter ships will hold eleven to a ship. Set your controls to engage and fire every five milations.

"Acazia, please show Raimee and Mary to the non-essentials waiting area; only fighter and key personnel allowed in this area. Your learning of Zenith provides experiencing many key aspects of the goings on, but this is off limits for now."

"Okay, thank you," Mary replies graciously.

Oris continues, "Set your fighter pod to a timed start. The launch order will be Pod Number 1-10 launching within three milations of each other."

∞

By nimilight, all fighter pods launch on their way to Meridius. Mary, Raimee, and several key Zenithians watch as the last of the ten ships disappear out of sight. There are no lights, no smoke, and no trail of any kind as proof of existence.

"How long does it take for them to reach Meridius?" Mary asks Friend. "It's as if the ships crept from Zenith," cracking a laugh. "I'm sure that is why you all call it a sneak attack, because you can't hear a sound coming from them."

"It takes approximately one zenot to arrive at the edge of Meridius."

"Is that all? It must not be very far from here."

"I'm not sure how far it is in distance, but it is quite a distance from Zenith. The ships travel extremely fast and can go a long distance within one zenot."

Mary's curiosity continues, "How do they know that firing every five minutes, I mean milations will bring about the desired result against Meridius?"

"The number of times to fire at a planet is a carefully planned process and has been used for years and during multiple attacks. Also attached onboard each ship is measurement equipment. Let's not talk about other planets anymore. The focus is now on Earth and its inhabitants," Acazia encouragingly remarks.

"One more question. Will the destruction of Earth be a factor that Xanthus is considering?"

"Raimee, that will be a question for Xanthus to determine."
Five milations outside of Meridius, the pods silently hover while ZAW's wait for instructions to act. Morik flips a switch, and an orange light appears.

Commander Xanthus spreads encouragement to the fight commanders, "Ready all ZAW leaders; prepare for engagement, and when prompted fire every five milations."

Zenithian fighters hurriedly, almost in unison place protective wear over their faces and heads; they placed protective gear to their bodies prior to arriving.

"We've done this many times before. Let's get it done; let's crush the threat and get back to Zenith–back to our lives."

He turns on the Kreto monitor and calls out, "Genus, Ruler of Meridius, hear me. This is Xanthus of Zenith. We are here in peace. It is not necessary to fight. Please take the opportunity to join and live together in harmony. There's so much we can do together with peace."

Genus coldly responds, "This is Meridius; we are and will always be Meridians. Never will we live in peace with Zenithians.

"Xanthus, I am ready," he states with an elevated and assured voice. "Do what you must. We like the way we live and will continue our way of life. Citizens of Meridius have free will to do as they please within reason."

"What's within reason?" is Xanthus' quick but calm comeback. "Ill treatment: unequal distribution of resources, assets, wealth, and certain citizens kept hostage by way of self importance, superiority, and entitlement. I'm sure that's not how Meridians view your definition of free will."

"Bear witness, we did not create havoc and declare war on Zenith when your soldiers attempted to accompany some Meridians to your Zenith. The Zenithian warriors had the audacity to step foot on Meridius and put out feelers for lost Meridians."

"One more time, I implore you Genus. It is a better life and best for all to join the peaceful union. Think of all the thousands of Meridians who look to your judgment for guidance in making the correct decision on behalf of your entire planet."

Xanthus waits for a response from Genus. Twenty milations pass, forty milations pass, with no response.

"Ready all pods; forty milations have past. Sixty milations, no response received."

Xanthus does a last minute check with the Warrior Commanders. "Are there any questions or problems?"

No answers from the ZAW leaders.

"No questions or problems, launch the nazum immediately," Xanthus orders.

Within quibs, each ship releases a thick blue fog; a mere three milations later the nazum lightly coats Meridius. The fighter ships move clockwise after three milations, continuing for two additional three milation rotations. Xanthus reminds the fighters to fire every five milations. The Zenithian fighters spray another blue layer.

∞

Curiously, Raimee's comments take the form of questions.

"It's been over two zenots since the ZAWs left. Where are the bombs, loud booms, blasts, or lasers? If it only takes one zenot, the fighting should have started. Do you think they're still going through with the plan?"

Friend remarks, "The only way Xanthus doesn't go through with it is if Meridius' leader agrees to the peaceful Zenithian way of life."

Raimee continues, "Are they using war methods shown on TV?"

"Xanthus' plan is to completely decimate everything on Meridius. The use of nazum, a thick blue fog, allows hands off war activity."

Keric delivers a reasonable explanation, "Xanthus will try to work it out with Meridius, or rather with Genus, the ruler of Meridius. Xanthus will never go to another realm or planet and strike without a last milation peace talk. Before making a final decision, Xanthus reaches out to the ruler of a realm many times for a peace plan. The objective is to get the ruler of another realm or planet to join us in peace and to treat all peoples with respect.

"Remember this is not the first contact with Meridius. Xanthus has talked, discussed, and tried to reason with Genus, the Meridian ruler on numerous occasions. This is the final encounter to beg for peaceful unity.

"It's always a plus that the powerful Xanthus is extremely intelligent. Remember he is GOD; it is the reason he is the GOD of Zenith. He knows all and can do anything. His intelligence, wisdom, and insight come natural. No need for book studies when birthed with so many wonderful gifts and talents. It's a better life and best for all to join in peace."

Viewing through the Kanwabe Raimee responds, "Oh my goodness, what is that stuff? I want to know. I have been waiting to hear loud noises and big booms throughout the air, but instead the air is quiet and misty blue."

"Acazia, Friend," Raimee curiously continues, "What is in that nazum? How did it clear out everything quickly and quietly?"

"It's a blue colored coating that is dispersed like a fog. Once the spraying of the nazum coating on a specific area or an entire planet, everywhere it lands disintegrates and dries up.

"It is a powerful war tool. The extraction of materials found on Zenith fashion into extremely effective weapons for destruction of an entire realm or planet. Workers dig for the material nimix. It is a necessary natural resource for Zenithian defense."

Acazia informs Raimee and Mary, "In thirty milations both of you can take another look through the Kanwabe. In all cases the water will dry up, the land will be barren, and the planet will be desolate."

∞

Fifteen milations later after the fog subsides Vonth and Ikee, along with eight other fighter ships hover Meridius. Each ship boasts an extremely large magnifier to view the planet for signs of life.

Commander Oris presses the button; Xanthus speaks to all ZAW's, "Within eighty to ninety additional milations unload; check Meridius for signs of life.

Three zenots later, "After carefully scouring the entire planet it appears that everything on Meridius is gone. All living matter, plant, animal, even water creatures are disintegrated."

∞

Raimee walks toward the entrance, and asks, "Excuse me, ah what's your name?" as a dark haired man in his 40's walks in.

"My name is Kriel. You are new to Zenith. What are your names? I forget, how long have you been with us?"

"Hi Kriel, I'm Mary and this is Raimee."

"Hello," Raimee adds. "We have been on Zenith for over two metres."

"How long have you all been looking at Earth?"

"We have monitored Earth for some time now."

Raimee continues the questioning, "How long is for some time now? I hope you like what you see. It is funny how the scientists on our Earth have been studying various planets such as the Moon and Mars. They have names for various other planets such as Pluto, Neptune, Saturn, and others. I have never heard or read about Zenith or Meridius."

"Zenith, Meridius, and planets other than the ones common to Earth can be seen using only a Kanwabe and only traveled to and fro using Heavus, other natural travel vessels, and specific made ships or pods.

"They believe Earthlings are the only beings alive. Yes as you say they have traveled to the Moon and now talks are about moving to Mars."

Raimee puts her two cents in, "I'll say it if you don't. Humans on Earth are so superficial and stuck on themselves, to think within the universe that only Earth has intelligent life. That's exactly how we are; but really it is the thought processes, actions, and decisions of a few who make the decisions for the majority."

"Earthlings are the ones that named the other planets familiar to them," Kriel explains. "The fact of the matter is the other planets are just that. They are names that Earthlings have given, but they are not the true names of these planets. There are life forms on many planets and realms."

ROLES AND RESPONSIBILITIES

Kriel explains, "We have long studied your life beings using the Zimeon Earth Test (ZET) to determine which EBOI to place on the observation list. Currently there are a number of EBOIs on the list but you ladies are the first Earthlings to actually study, make contact, and reveal ourselves."

"What's an EBOI?" Mary continues asking eagerly. "An eboy," with a slight chuckle.

"It's an Earth Being of Interest," Acazia responds proudly. "It's you and Raimee. It's for us, what you have been for some time."

"An Earth Being of Interest, I still need more information."

Kriel steps in to offer further explanation, "Mary, Acazia is correct. We did not pull the two of you out of a hat. There are procedures to follow. First, carefully choose an EBOI. Before selecting you as our EBOI the Zenith Upper Guardians spent countless lunas reviewing lives of many Earthlings nimix living. The next step is to assign Zenithian helpers and support. All Zenithian roles eventually travel to Earth to support the EBOI, like Friend and Acazia have done for you and Raimee.

"There are a number of supporters assigned to each EBOI. The next step after choosing an EBOI is to select a Special Assigned Guardian (SAG).

As the name suggests this designation is of most importance to the EBOI. The Special Assigned Guardian's basis of assignment depends on several rating factors including compatibility and the highest percentage of a successful friendship and personal relationship. They have learned how to develop and become friends, mentors, teachers, and protectors for their EBOI. It is an important role. SAGs must gain the trust of the EBOI assignment. It is not a fake relationship, but a true one between a Special Assigned Guardian and an Earth Being of Interest. The goal is for them to develop a trusting relationship and for the SAG to learn as much as possible in order to help make the EBOI's life easier on Earth. Therefore, SAGs need outstanding personal, mental, sympathetic, and empathetic mindsets, which make them the ideal support system. The start of this friendship/relationship is critical and crucial to the success and outcome of each scheduled mission.

Acazia and Friend are SAGs assigned to each of you. There are other Zenithians training and many others eager to train for the role of SAG. It is one of the top assignments on Zenith. Also reviewing of the next selection of EBOIs is ongoing.

"That is why Zenith Upper Guardians give SAGs the opportunity, if available, to select their EBOI.

Zenith Upper Guardian (ZUG) - a Zenithian advisor chosen by Xanthus to oversee the selection of SAG to an EBOI, to review, and report everything back to Xanthus.

"Next, assignment to the EBOI is a Touran. Tourans are lookouts that assist with the monitoring as it relates to the EBOI. The Tourans role is very important as SAGS depend on their monitoring skills to support and achieve the goals set forth for the EBOI. The SAG selects the Tourans assigned to an EBOI and report to the SAG. Tincher and Hemi are Tourans (lookouts) assigned to each of you.

"Special Earth Assignment (SEA) - Reemy and Kravon are SEAs assigned to both of you. Unlike a SAG (Special Assigned Guardian), a SEA (Special Earth Assignment) rarely participates in every aspect of an EBOI's life. A SEA receives a special request for the assigned EBOI. A Special Earth Assignment (SEA) must travel to Earth immediately after the SAG assignment to an EBOI and before the SAG travels to Earth. The SAG gives the SEA the special request. In most cases, a SEA will have multiple special requests per SAG. A SEA must have the ability to manage several special requests at the same time.

The SEA is selected by and reports to the SAG.

"CORDERS - keep logs of communications and everyday happenings with the EBOI. The logs are visual and audio, not written. Alliodd and Ivan are Corders assigned to each of you. This role is of the utmost importance. CORDERS keep everything that happens relating to an EBOI as proof. It is a way for the EBOI supporters to research and study their EBOI along with the people and situations in their life. CORDERS must possess the capabilities to have a photographic (visual and auditory) memory. This allows the reporting of all things happening nimix of an EBOI's life captured and transferred to the SAG without a written trail within the CORDER. The information although captured not saved; therefore, after each

transfer of information to the SAG the CORDER has an internal function nimix automatically clears all captured video and audio data, allowing each time to capture and transfer the new data received.
CORDERS are selected by and reports to the SAG.

"Guardian Assist Support (GAS) - helpers so things run smoother. On Earth, you would call them a personal assistant. Caton, Valora, and Damus are GAS assigned to each of you. The assignment goes for the EBOI, but mostly assists other roles to run smoother and put out any fires as necessary. SAG, SEA, Touran, and CORDER as a team, review and select the Guardian Assist Support. Although the Guardian Assist Support (GAS) role is to assist all roles, they report to the SAG.

"Cherites - A Cherites role is to visit an EBOI in their dreams. The EBOI's dreams are premonitions, whether good or bad and subject to adherence. The premonitions become more frequent and stronger as the EBOI's experiences increase or change. Cherites only place dreams that are beneficial to the EBOI. The EBOI's dream may be positive or negative. It may make them happy or sad; it shows them what is going to happen and gives them a visual, whether good or bad, and who may have an impact on their life.
Cherites communicate with all other roles as a basis for determining what dreams to place with the EBOI.
Selecting Cherites for specific EBOIs falls to Xanthus. and await their EBOI assignment. Whichever Cherite is next in line is assigned to an EBOI. Torza and Satera are Cherites assigned to each of you. EBOI's receive all roles at an early age, usually before early teens; some as soon as pre-tweens.
Cherites spend more time on Earth than any other assigned role.

"Zenith Allegiant Warrior (ZAW) - are dedicated, loyal, and unwavering. Zenith warriors pledge their dying allegiance to Xanthus and to Zenith. In addition, ZAWs begin training at the age of ten on the art of being a true warrior, respect, honor, and what being a Zenithian means to all. Zenithian Allegiant Warriors are chosen by Xanthus and the ZAW training teams."

Raimee asks Xanthus, "Have you ever had any contact with Earth beings away from Zenith? If so, how do you present yourself?"

"As Xanthus, GOD, my presence on Zenith is through a physical appearance. When visiting Earth it is always through the spirit and revealed only through voice and spirit. The flesh of my physical body does not reveal to inhabitants from other planets and realms until they reach Zenith. Zenithians and visitors to Zenith are able to see, hear, touch, and communicate with me."

Raimee continues questioning Xanthus, "How long have you been researching and analyzing us? I really want to know how you decided to choose me. What did I do to warrant this special treatment? Help me to understand."

Xanthus responds, "As previously disclosed your lives have been studied for many lunas. The time is finally right to reveal ourselves, who we are, our belief system, plans for you and Mary, and to share it all."

"I thank you for intervening in my life. I cannot speak for anyone else but the timing is great. My life is so depressing. I was giving up. What do you know? I had no idea a person by the name of Lakeeda would change my life forever. Thank you all for bringing me to this place of love. I know I have a long way to go and must continue all the training and pass the testing; I will try and give all that I have to be pleasing to you, GOD Xanthus."

"I know you will Raimee. We all know both you and Mary will excel and that will please us; I'm sure it will please each of you."

Raimee acknowledges, "I know Acazia and Friend are goddesses. How many other goddesses are there? How many other Gods are there?"

Acazia answers, "There are other GODs. Xanthus is the GOD for all Zenithians. Other GODs have specific roles. All Goddesses have specific roles. The Mother Goddess for all Goddesses and Zenithians shall be Xanthus' chosen mate."

ZAPP

Every other nimi Mary and Raimee attend ZAPP training. The nimis not attending they participate in nimix activities missed while in training such as sharing chores, researching, cooking, and keeping the planet clean. There are many duties and tasks required to assist in reaching the goals for Zenith. On the nimis Mary and Raimee perform planet clean-up duties they can view a lot more of Zenith.

∞

Four metres have passed; Raimee and Mary are half the way through ZAPP training. A massive amount of knowledge of Zenith is learned.

Acazia, Friend, and Xanthus are in the process of helping to determine Mary and Raimee's talents and abilities. A determination of their talents and abilities allows the assignment of their roles and responsibilities.

∞

A total of eight metres have passed.

Meta knocks on their door.

"Come in Meta," Mary states while exhibiting a great deal of friendship.

Raimee greets him without turning or glancing his way.

"Hi ladies, I have something for you." Meta hands a slip of paper to Mary.

She flips open the folded notice and reveals a mandatory invitation for her and Raimee to attend a function two nimis from now.

The dress is tastefully casual.

∞

Zenithians, including all of Raimee's and Mary's support roles and Xanthus stand in the front area of the assembly. All appear happy.

Lorga, ZAPP trainer, conveys their accomplishments, "Your ZAPP training is complete. I want to thank you for participating. It's been a pleasure to work with the both of you, and I could not have wished for better students."

Xanthus stands at the speaker area, and Lorga steps back, "You have completed a special program. Congratulations!"

Mary and Raimee stand and walk toward the speaker's area. Xanthus remains; Acazia and Friend stand beside him. All their support roles crowd around the speaker's area.

Raimee shares, "I am extremely happy, extremely grateful, and want to thank everyone." She tries to shake everyone's hand.

Mary shares, "I thank all of you for helping." She begins to shake each hand.

The assembly stands, raises their right arm straight up, and bends it up and down, exhibiting the Zenith sign of peace. "Mary and Raimee, Mary and Raimee, Mary and Raimee," ring out from the mouths of the Zenithian audience showing their support.

"Everything has been a great learning experience. I truly enjoyed it," Raimee exclaims.

"Now, are you prepared? I hope so, because today you are going to test on what you have learned during the entire eight metres of training. The test lasts for three zenots straight. Both of you have two zenots to rest and return to this room."

"Will you be the one to test us?" Mary questions their trainer, Lorga.

She shakes her head, "No it won't be me."

"Awe, why not? We have spent eight metres together. I like you."

"It has been a great eight metres and I too enjoyed the time spent with you and Raimee. The Evaluators will determine if either of you are mentally, emotionally, and physically ready to reenter society; to determine if you're ready to be rid of the shackles, pain, hurt, humiliation, and inferiority thrust upon you, to let it go, to see what the

Zenithians have shown you. The evaluator's name is Tanzeer. Again take about two zenots for a break and return back."

∞

Upon returning in time for the testing, Mary heads toward the snack area.

Raimee yells, "I'm going to use the restroom. Three zenots is a long time."

"They should let us go to the bathroom if there is a need."

"Probably. But just in case, I'm going now." She runs toward the bathroom.

"You are probably right. I should go. Hold up, wait for me."

"Hurry, we only have a total of fifteen milations until test time."

Two and one-fourth zenots later, after the written portion of the test is complete, Raimee is moving to another area to commence the verbal test.

"Will you discuss what ZAPP training is to you?"

"Yes, I'd be happy to try."

Mary continues the written portion for the remaining three fourth zenot. Once the remaining three fourth zenot has lapsed, she will begin the verbal test.

Raimee stands to her feet and continues, "Okay, I'll start with saying, no this place is not a cult. At the beginning, I really thought you all were something like a cult. There are many so-called cults–people living a life separate and different from the majority, the status quo. They are considered a cult. The life on Zenith is so unique with structured and non-structured activities.

"Being on Zenith and a part of this world makes me feel okay. I am accepted and allowed to be the person I was born and intended to be. I have never had that feeling on Earth.

"Living, no existing on Earth is one of the worse things a person like me can experience.

"I don't feel displaced. Even though I am not accustomed to this life, it is such a good feeling. I feel part of something. Here we are not considered different or weird. The funny thing is that we look so much different from the Zenithians, but I feel much more alive and happy. I am not made to feel inferior, isolated, and alone. I have found PEACE, the peace Earth is not able and cannot provide me. It feels like home."

"It is a good feeling," Mary says. "I want my family to feel this good."

"We understand and believe in both of you, even when you don't understand or believe in yourselves. This is what it's all about," Xanthus encouragingly remarks. "All of this is done and the choosing of you two shows our belief in you for some time."

Raimee starts crying, "I can't believe it. I've waited so long for someone to understand me; I've waited for someone to truly see the person no other has seen, and I've waited for someone to care about me as the person I am or am not. I can be me and not be judged, shunned, or made to feel I am not a part of something. I do not have to feel inferior to everyone. I am finally in a clique."

∞

Raimee shares, "Most of the time I am not happy, struggling with financial, emotional, mental, and physical woes.

"People with money and mostly power often try to break a person in as many ways as possible. Pleasure can be derived from the act of placing another life in harm's way. I can't just say it is only people with money and power, because plenty of plain and poor folk sure have tried to break me as well. I have probably dealt with many of both in my personal and professional life.

"There is so much unnecessary sickness, crime, and negative happenings affecting one's life. Many are made to feel inferior by those in the minority who claim to be superior and who place an undue hardship and societal burden on the majority considered inferior either by lack of resources (financial, mental, emotional, human, support, lineage and luck), or human inflicted factors.

"When life is so unfair by so many factors there is no wonder so many illnesses and diseases plague our existence."

GIFTS

After the assembly, all Zenithians leave. An escort takes Mary and Raimee back to their rooms; Acazia and Friend stay behind for a discussion with Xanthus.

Xanthus remarks, "I see life changes in both ladies. It is explosive and at the same time very calming. Both ladies have come a long way. I have something to give you for their return home. It's time their lives on Earth are a little easier."

"What is it?" Friend asks.

"I'm giving you a vial."

He hands Friend and Acazia each a vial.

"As soon as you get off Heavus, you will need to release contents of the vial into the air. It needs fulfilled without either ladies knowledge. The important thing to remember is it must be done by night fall the nimi of your return to Earth to be completely effective."

Dutiful Friend holds her vial up above her head, squinting hard to view the contents. She inquires, "What's in it GOD Xanthus; what is its purpose? I don't see anything. There is no noise, like a liquid sound when I shake it, no sound at all."

Acazia holds her vial out in front of her.

"This is the first time we will have successfully sent two beings back to Earth. Raimee and Mary have been here for a period receiving training from unexpected and to them, unusual beings. The vials contain the keys to bringing both the type of life they long for and deserve. Once the content reaches the air, you will see how society relates to them. It will be so beautiful."

"What is the proper way to release the contents into the air?" Friend questions.

"Once the vial is opened a small maze located on the ground will appear, only visible to the two of you. Aim the vial at the beginning point, allowing the contents to flow until empty. Once the vial is opened and is aimed downwards, the content drains out quickly.

Xanthus continues, "Also, they won't have recollection of how Earth's society has previously mistreated and abused them. They won't know what hit them, but you can believe they will enjoy the outcomes to be received from two small vials."

"Why are they unable to recall past mistreatment and abuse? We want them to change?"

"Yes, we do Friend; but in a positive way, not negative at all. The remnants of past relationship traumas can undermine success from programming they have completed. This is the reason we must continue to support their transition upon returning to Earth. The impacts and outcomes that affect them will need to be monitored and reported."

"What are some of the negative things you're talking about?"

"You must monitor them at all times. All support assigned to each of them will be located on Earth to assist and keep you informed. We need to know how this affects them and how they react to the changes in their lives. Each of you will report to me. Therefore, it is imperative your support team is on the ball performing their jobs and assignments with quality outcomes."

Acazia acknowledges; she comprehends Xanthus' explanation, "You want to help them but also want to analyze whether they truly are the Earthlings we chose, monitored, loved, and brought to Zenith. I understand, don't you Friend?"

"Yes, I do understand."

"Their memories of you as Sasha and Friend, Lakeeda, and Acazia will remain intact."

"How will the memories of Acazia and me remain?"

He wants them to understand, "The reason their memories of the two of you will remain is their interactions with you, Sasha, Lakeeda, and Acazia were always positive, loving, and helpful. Only negative interactions, relationships, mistreatment, and abuse will be wiped away."

∞

"They won't understand why their lives have changed, but it is definitely for the positive.

"It is important that you share yourself with them in several forms. You still need to be Sasha, Friend, Lakeeda, and Acazia. And you will need to become several others.

"After the good things start coming their way I want to see if and how they react, if they change themselves or if they remain the same. I want you to approach them as a person with less than good character. I want you to continue to earn their trust. It should be easy since you are true to them and love them. You will know other relationships you need based on the circumstances that arise; use your best judgment.

"Situations will arise and the both of you will need to be ready. As you know, we must not allow either Raimee or Mary to learn the truth about the new faces you will become."

RETURN EARTH

Friend announces, "It is time for you to go back to Earth; it's time for us to go back to Earth. Acazia and I will accompany both of you on your return trip.

"Yes, I'm happy." Mary claps. "I get to see my mom and brothers. Mom has probably been worried; I know her personality."

"I am glad also. I truly miss my son. I'm also very glad that both of you are traveling back with us."

Friend continues, "Have you gotten all your items ready to take back with you?"

∞

Three nimis later Friend informs the ladies during lunch, "We are leaving tomorrow.

"Are you ready? Everything is complete for the time being on Zenith. Once you return to Earth, your new lives need to stand the test of time.

"The ZAPP training completed on Zenith will be in place on Earth when you return. Acazia and I will monitor your activities to see how things progress. You have been away from Earth and living the life of another planet of beings. Eight metres is a long time to be away with no contact."

Doting Zenithians show great spirits.

"Meta, Acazia, and I will load your things and drop you off where you will spend your last night on Zenith."

Mary and Raimee receive escorts to an even lovelier part of Zenith than was previously experienced.

Dazzling waterfalls change colors as they walk. First fuchsia, electric blue, and lavender spill into a contained pond. Directly across another waterfall with the same changing colors also spill into the same contained pond. Up jumps what looks like a salmon colored fish. It is so big that Mary jumps back with a slight shrill, although, it may be the color rather than the size that startled her.

"Did it scare you Mary?" Acazia asks.

"Yeah, just for a moment. It mostly startled me."

Raimee shares her lovely thoughts, "Everything is so colorful. Bright and pastel flowers surround the lovely buildings, the colorful walkways, and green space; everything is so neat and clean. This is what happens when a realms total population takes pride in its appearance and work regularly to keep it a beautiful, refuse free place to live."

"Another nimilight gone and bedtime is near," Mary says to Raimee. "Zenith is so beautiful. We've been treated extremely well. I can't wait to wake up in the morning to see my family."

"We have learned some valuable tools to empower ourselves. Byron will be a blessing to my eyes."

∞

Morning arrives; Mary is up and showered before the alarm clock rings.

She calls out, "Raimee get up, Raimee get up."

Eyeing Mary, Raimee stretches and yawns, "Wow, you're ready to roll. While I shower please put some coffee on. Thanks!"

Forty-five milations later Friend and Acazia go to Raimee and Mary's door and are ready to leave, "Come on ladies, it's time," Friend reminds them.

A few quibs later and all four women are out the door. In an instance a beautiful rainbow appears.

Friend holds out her arm and boasts a smile, "Your chariot waits."

The four ladies walk onto Heavus; all of them have smiles plastered on their face. The appearance of happiness is abundantly clear.

"Earth here we come. We are ready, so hold on," Raimee admits.

Mary laughs and says, "We look like the four musketeers." They all laugh. "I'm ready to see mom and my brothers. I miss them so much." A tear dribbles from the corner of each of her beautiful brown eyes. She sniffles, noticing us noticing her. She softly explains, "These are happy tears."

Raising her eyebrows, "Don't you like being with us?" Friend asks.

"Of course I love being with you. Being the four musketeers has been the highlight for me. The past eight metres have been so wonderful."

Raimee chimes in, "Yeah, I love being with the both of you and being around all our new family and friends on Zenith. I have found a new world in which I have needed my entire life. Nothing I have experienced on Earth will ever compare. I hope everything works out and someday I will be able to come back to Zenith with my son by my side. I will be wishing for it.

"If I didn't know it to be true, I would think I have been dreaming this entire time. Now that we are away from Zenith, the idea of going back to Earth is settling in and it is not a good feeling. The only thing helpful is to know I will see my son.

"We are almost there; Byron here I come darling.

"I found out there is so much love out there. You all helped me find it. You let me be who I am meant to be; you made me stronger and gave me back myself. I don't want to sound mushy, really I don't. I have gone from always being treated inferior in everything to being respected as me, my capabilities, with unconditional acceptance."

"Don't worry about it Raimee," Acazia reassures her in a comforting voice. "You've had your share of negative experiences on Earth. Even though you have completed the ZAPP training, it is not unusual to have some uncomfortable feelings and thoughts about the place in your programming. The main thing is to get past that and not harbor those feelings and thoughts. Let them go. I am here to help; Friend is also here, along with other Zenithian support. Everything will be okay.

"Remember the purpose of the training. Hold your gracious head high; once we reach Earth you will see and experience the transformation that awaits you."

Mary adds, "Thank you Acazia and Friend. I can't wait for the experience. The word transformation sounds so good to my ears."

Raimee settles in closing her eyes and propping up her head. She smiles and says, "Even without a pillow or blanket this is relaxing." She does a grunt-like laugh and continues, "Don't wake me if you hear snoring."

Snickering, Mary replies, "I'm gonna pinch you." She sighs, "I guess I'll try and rest myself." Within ten quibs she starts talking again but with an inside voice.

"Here we go ladies; no more talking. Sit back, rest your bodies, and mind. Once you fall asleep we will be back on Earth before you know it."

"We have gone so far already. Zenith has disappeared as if it never was; I can't see it anymore–it's just a memory," Mary exclaims. "Thanks, and I know you say to rest. I agree; I just can't quit talking about and sharing my feelings."

Raimee begs to know, "Is it all real and everything is as beautiful and wonderful as it's supposed to be; not just the physical beauty of Zenith, but the beauty of emotional and mental attributes?

"After being hurt so much and experiencing pain for so many years by everybody all the time, it is hard for me. I know you understand. Do not stop being here, there, and everywhere. I need you more than ever. Now that my new family has come into my life I will seek out unconditional love."

Mary reaches out her arms and makes an air embrace to Friend and to Acazia. By the time she air embraces Raimee, a tear rolls down her face. "I love you all."

Afterwards, everything settles down; Raimee and Mary are sleep.

∞

Finally, Heavus reaches Earth, gently gliding in around 1:00 p.m. The sky shows as a beautiful rainbow.

"In Earth measurements the trip took approximately twenty-six hours. Not bad considering our travels was from outer space," Friend says.

The four musketeers are back. Mary, Raimee, Friend, and Acazia walk off Heavus in that order.

"We made it. Halleluiah," Mary happily exclaims!

Raimee asks, "Is the rainbow visible to others? I wonder if someone saw us unload off Heavus. You know it will be the talk of the town and everyone will try to have a piece of it."

Acazia reassures the ladies, "This is the reason to not spill the beans too soon. Let us accustom both of you back to Earth and we will go from there. Okay?"

∞

Mary holds her head down.

"Did you spill the beans about Friend and Acazia?" The expression on Mary's face alerts Raimee of what she has done. "What did you do? Did you tell your family? We were told not to let anyone, even family know about our special friends and our trip to Zenith. What if your family talks to other people?"

"I'm not sure; I'm hoping they don't blab."

"All we can do is to beg your family to keep quiet."

RELEASE THE GIFT

S itting in the grass Mary turns around; she eyes Raimee, next Acazia, and lastly Friend. Raimee, Friend, and Acazia sit with her. "I guess we should call you Sasha and Lakeeda. There is no better time to start than now."

A big smile on Mary's face as she tilts her head back and stares up into the sky. "Friend, my friend, isn't the sky so beautiful and blue?"

Friend, Raimee, and Acazia all peer upward at the same time.

"Ooh," Raimee said. "Yes Mary, it's really pretty."

"Was the sky gray after we unloaded from Heavus?"

Raimee answers, "It was dull and gray; now it's a myriad of vibrant colors."

"What is the first thing you will do?" Acazia asks the ladies.

Raimee quickly responds, "See my son and get some rest."

"See my mom and brothers," Mary adds.

∞

Acazia and Friend lock hands with Mary and Raimee pulling both ladies close to them,

"Give us a big hug."

Raimee says, "The sky is gray again."

As all four embrace, Acazia and Friend, unaware to Raimee and Mary, with their thumb flip open the vial given them by Xanthus, and release a liquid upon the ground. Acazia and Friend simultaneously embrace them in opposite view of the vial release. Friend and Acazia look toward each other, waiting for the contents to show; it is not flowing. As soon as they gaze at each other the liquid, a milky blue color quickly spreads around the four ladies, meets to form a circle, then rises above to the gray sky. They are none the wiser. Neither is aware of what just occurred.

I'M HOME

All of them walk two blocks to the rental car lot.
Mary chimes in, "A rental car; good looking out Friend."
Inside the car rental agency Acazia and Friend select a Chrysler 300M. "Chrysler 300M is a very nice car; Chrysler makes good-looking vehicles. It makes sense to get the 300M and take advantage of the special monthly rental." Acazia pays for the rental. "Eventually I may buy a vehicle."

Mary is driven home as the first stop.

Raimee, Acazia, and Friend respectively express to Mary, "Have a good night Mary, goodnight, and night."

Stepping foot on the porch she turns, "Thanks, see you all tomorrow." Her mom, ready to give her a big hug and kiss, walks into the house, greets Mary with arms wide-open and puckered lips.

"My baby girl is finally home. Baby I missed you so much and I want to hear all about your all girl's trip. It has been eight months. The time felt about right. You originally told me eight months, so I followed the calendar, marking what your estimated return date would be. My count was off by only one day. I calculated you returning tomorrow. One day early is completely fine by me."

"Hi, I missed you too mommy, but I'm so tired. Let me take my things to the bedroom and lie down for a sec. I'll come back and tell you all about it. Where are my brothers?"

"Go on and take a nap; I will make sure they are here when you get up. They will be glad you are back and will want to see you."

She blows a hand kiss, "Thanks mom, I love you."

She heads toward her bedroom makes a stop in the bathroom, and she thinks, *I need to take a shower but I'm so tired; me just want to lie down and go to sleep.* Heading back toward her bedroom and trying to reason with herself. *No, I had better take one now.*
After a brief shower, she climbs into bed and within minutes is snoring.

Ms. Sutton dials the phone. "Malcolm, where are you? Your sister is home and I want you to come here right away. Did you speak to your brother? Call and tell him to make it home as soon as possible."

"He's here with me mom. Have you cooked or do I need to pick up something?"

"If you and your brother don't mind I plan to cook."

"Okay mom, we'll be there soon."

"Okay dear."

∞

Fifteen minutes later the rental car pulls up in Raimee's driveway. Raimee unloads and Acazia and Friend get out.

"My key is not readily available. I'll knock on the door; Byron will let us in."

Knocking, Knocking and no Byron have come to the door.

Raimee finally finds her key and opens the door. She enters the house and flicks on the light switch. "Oh my, the house is clean."

Acazia and Friend walk in, "Nice place Raimee."

"Thanks! Ladies look around and learn the house. This is also your place until you find something."

Raimee continues to check around. Something is different. He moved a few things in the living room, switched the TV with the couch and chairs.

"I have an extra bedroom with two beds. Please make yourselves at home and while you are getting comfy, I will get some food in here. Towels and washcloths are in the bathroom closet. Liquid soap is in the shower. Please help yourself. And again, please make yourself at home. Do not act like guests; act like this is your home also. Byron should be here soon. I am calling him now."

Raimee calls Byron with the biggest smile on her face, "Hi honey, it's your mom. I'm home."

"Hey mom, I'm on my way; see you in fifteen."

"Take your time honey, don't rush. I will be here."

Before he hangs up, she quickly says, "Oh honey, we have company. My two friends are staying here while they're visiting."

"Okay make it twenty minutes. Is there anything I need to bring home?"

"No sweetheart–I'm calling in an order to be delivered."

"Take your time honey; do not rush. I will be here."

Twenty minutes later Byron drives up, walks in the house, straight to give his mom a hug. He squeezes her tight, slightly lifting her off the floor. "Hey mom, I missed you so much. Eight months is a long time to be on a vacation and be away from your loving son."

"Sweetheart, I missed you terribly," tears gently roll down her face.

"Where's your company? Who is it? Do I know them?"

234

"It is Sasha and Lakeeda. They are probably resting. I put them in the room with the two beds; let us not bother them. Just you and I can do some catching up. I will talk about my time away and experiences. You can tell me how things went while staying with your aunt. Sound like a winner?"

∞

"To be honest mom, I wish you were here. There are things I needed from my mother. Eight months is a long time to depend on others. It is not the same as when you look after me."

"But Byron, honey you are old enough to help take care of yourself. When I was your age I took care of a child, you, and worked a full-time job."

"Mom, what are you saying? It sounds like you think I should not put any blame on you."

"That is exactly what I think."

"Okay look honey, we need to push back and calm down. You are my dear son, and I love you to pieces. Arguing is the last thing I expect to happen when we saw each other.

"Please honey, I love you."

TOGETHER AGAIN

Yeah mom you are right. Tell me all about your trip. Tell me everything. You tell me about your adventures and I am going to discuss mine. I can't wait to hear about it all."

"Well son, it happened like this. Remember me telling you that Mary and I planned to visit a foreign planet called Zenith with Lakeeda and Sasha. That is where I have been this entire time. We traveled on what they call Heavus, but on Earth we call it a rainbow."

Byron is surprised, eyebrows raised, and head tilted slightly to the side.

"I met Xanthus, the GOD of ZENITH and another world of beings called Zenithians. Mary and I had the best time. They treated us especially well. We learned a lot about their beliefs and way of life. Now we are back. The entire time there, eight months was dedicated to learning about Zenith."

Byron sighed. He slowly moved his fore and middle finger across the top of his brow. He glanced down and then up and said, "Wait a minute mom, slow way down; you went to another planet, a realm. You actually traveled away from Earth on a rainbow?"

He stared his mom straight in the eyes. He waited for her to say, I am sorry honey; I played with you. However, she did not. She stood steadfast to her story.

"I know it sounds weird honey and hard to believe, but it's true. Do you believe me? Honey, I truly want you to know in your heart your mom told you facts and not made up stories."

"Yeah mom, I believe you. Do you have Heavus lag?" he asked as he held back a snicker. "Sorry mom; I just couldn't resist."

"Don't laugh my dear son, because it's true. You will find out eventually just how true it actually is. Friend and Acazia, you know them as Sasha and Lakeeda, initially told us that we could not discuss with anybody. So, we didn't. Do you know how hard it is to keep secrets from you? It is extremely hard that was because we always share everything. Finally opening up and sharing with you feels good."

∞

Mary joins her mom and two brothers in the living room for dinner and TV. "We're about to eat; it's been eight months since all four of us ate a meal together. I love it and I love you all."

"Mom, Bobby, and Malcolm, I hope you believe me because what I am going to say is true. Raimee and I have been gone all this time visiting a place called Zenith. It's a faraway place and the only way to get there is through a rainbow called Heavus."

"How far away?" Bobby asks.

Malcolm sarcastically replies, "You mean the rainbow that shows up in the sky after it rains? What did you call it, Heavus?

"So does that mean you can only travel when it rains?"

At the same time, all heads turn to eyeball Mary; Malcolm, Bobby, and Ms. Sutton glance at each other, stunned at what they hear. Malcolm pretends to clean his ears out as if he does not hear correctly.

"Yep, that's what I mean. I am saying our travels were on a rainbow and it was so smooth. I cannot wait to go again. The people there are so nice and treat us extremely well. They really like me; they like Raimee also."

"So you are saying aliens are nice and treat you good? And how do you know they like you; did they tell you?"

"Actually, they informed us both that they like us and we are family to them.

"Guess what else. There was a war while on Zenith."

"What type of war? This is getting interesting," Bobby proclaims.

"Zenith, the realm I was on, destroyed this other realm called Meridius."

"Did Zenith take the other planet as slaves?"

"No, they allow those who want to come peacefully to do so. Those choosing to follow Zenith become respectful parts of the family. The realm, Meridius exists no longer."

Ms. Sutton eyeballs Malcolm and Bobby. Motioning with her finger and silently lip talking the words,
"Don't misbehave; leave your sister alone."

CONTAGIOUS

Ten o'clock pm, a knock is at the front door. Everyone is asleep in the Sutton house. Malcolm has headphones on, Bobby's cd is playing, Mary's TV is watching her, and Ms. Sutton fell asleep in her bed flipping through a magazine.

Another set of knocks on the door and nobody answers.

A third set of knocks bring Mary out of her room, "Who is it?"

A voice from the other side of the door asks, "Mary Sutton is that you?"

"Yes, who's asking?"

"It's Dr. Zuir with the Parasitic Research Division of the Israel Medical Facility. May we come in?"

"Hold on." She runs to wake Ms. Sutton, "Mom, wake up, the doctor is at the door."

Sleepily Ms. Sutton wraps a robe around her and heads to the front room and peeks through the peephole.

"It's Dr. Zuir with the Israel Medical Facility."

"Dr. Zuir, what can we do for you?" Ms. Sutton asks as she offers him a seat.

"Sorry to disturb you so late for a night visit; I contacted Ms. Alexander and will visit her when we leave here. I do have some news to give you. Mary, where have you been for the past eight months? Our offices, doctors, and staff are truly concerned after not being able to reach you or Ms. Alexander. Numerous messages were left but no return calls received."

Dr. Zuir finally sits down on the cozy single chair.

∞

He explains, "We must take Mary along with Ms. Alexander to a quarantine facility."

Barely getting the words out, "Why, when?" Ms. Sutton questions.

"The doctors have the conclusion what each have is a parasite. We are not sure if it is contagious. The ladies have been unavailable for the past eight months. The protocol is quarantine the infected, along with those who were exposed. Take Mary and Raimee to the same quarantine location to be tested. Raimee and Mary need to be away from the public until the parasite they have is not contagious to others. Someone will keep you updated."

QUARANTINE

Mary, with an understandable expression of fright responds, "You can't do this. There's an explanation."

Mary and Ms. Sutton sit side by side and glance at each other. Mary asks, "What now?"

Dr. Zuir guides Mary's arm to the truck waiting outside. Two assistants climb from the truck, each taking Mary by an arm.

"Wait Dr. Zuir let me explain. Mom, Bobby," she cries out in an elevated voice.

"Wait I'm coming," Ms. Sutton anxiously yells.

"Sorry ma'am, but quarantine doesn't allow visitors."

"We're not visitors, we are family; I'm her mother."

"I understand, but not even family."

"How long will she be gone?"

"It depends; currently there is not a specific timeframe."

Mary sadly steps into the back of the truck, waving bye, tears flowing.

Dr. Zuir continues, "Let's head out to pick up Ms. Alexander."

∞

Fifteen minutes later, the truck pulls up to Raimee's house. Byron answers the knock at the door. Gazing past the man, he scopes the truck.

"Hi, I'm Dr. Zuir. Is Ms. Raimee Alexander home?"

"Wait here," Byron tells Dr. Zuir. "Mom, there is a doctor here to see you."

Raimee calmly walks in the living room through to the front door, "May I help you?"

"I'm with The Parasitic Research Facility. Since you and Ms. Sutton have been MIA for eight months, we are legally taking the two of you to quarantine. Please come with us now."

"Why?" Raimee cautiously asks.

Dr. Zuir, with haste, reveals, "The doctor's conclusion of what you and Mary have is a parasite. They want to place you and Ms. Sutton in quarantine until it is determined the parasite is not contagious."

Byron quickly interjects, "I'm coming with you. Wait until I get my clothes and shoes on."

"No family members allowed. No need to bring clothes; we will supply you with everything you need."

Byron is freaking out. He says, "That's not right. Why ya'll come in the middle of the night and take people out of their homes?"

Raimee quickly instructs him, "Wake up Sasha and Lakeeda. Inform them of the situation. Hurry now."

She steps inside the truck; Mary is sitting, no restraints, crying hysterically. Inside the truck, Raimee calms Mary. "Sasha and Lakeeda will know what to do; try not to worry."

Raimee asks, "Dr. Zuir, how long of a drive is it to where you are taking us?"

"Approximately one hour and fifty-five minutes."
Raimee continues trying to calm Mary.

Mary says, "Forty-five minutes have already passed. We will be at the quarantine place soon. I'm still worried."

"Mary, I have tried encouraging you not to worry. Keep the faith."

∞

Forty-five minutes later Dr. Zuir, his medics, Mary and Raimee drive to the hospital parking in an emergency spot.

Lightning strikes once, lightning strikes a second time. The sky turns an electric blue. Raimee and Mary are driving down the road with Lakeeda and Sasha. Mary is bobbing her head to the CD player.

With a puzzled look on his face, Dr. Zuir turns toward the medics. He asks, "Why are we out joy riding in the emergency medical vehicle? If we planned to go joy riding we should have taken the Cadillac Escalade."

"Okay Doc, let's call it a night; see you all tomorrow," one medic replies.

MESSAGE WAITING

A s the sun barely peeks through the bedroom drapes, Raimee slightly opens her eyes to blinking lights.
It is the answering machine. There are messages waiting.

Yeah, she is still old fashioned with a separate answering machine sitting on the bedroom table.

Slowly rising, wiping her eyes she slides her feet into bedroom slippers, glances at the answering machine, and pushes the play message button heading toward the bathroom. *Who has called me since yesterday?*

You have thirty-nine new messages the machine informs her. The first message begins to play.

She runs to her son's bedroom, "Byron, sweetie wake up."
Byron gets up and walks to his mother's room.

"Guess what? I have messages on the machine inviting me to attend special events. Listen to this one."

"Raimee Alexander, this is Randolph Trent requesting your presence at the Eighth Annual Celebrity Gala in Atlanta. A limo will pick up you and a plus one next Thursday at 7:00 p.m. The event will begin the following Saturday at 4 o'clock p.m. Please say yes. Call me at 778-648-0001 for more details and your answer. Thank you."

With more excitement in her voice, "Okay here's another message."

"Ms. Raimee, I've learned you are a basketball fan. Season Box Seat tickets have been reserved for you to attend the Charlotte Murans. You can bring four additional people. Contact my assistant at 1-822-100-6100 with details of your plans to attend and how many will be with you. Thanks."

"Listen to this; it's the craziest one so far."

"Ms. Raimee Alexander, we want you to visit. You and two others can fly to each of the following destinations, Africa, China, Spain, Rome, India, and Egypt. Call for additional instructions at 1-800-401-2001. And by the way the trips are separate, so you have the ability if you so desire, to take two different guests with you on each trip."

"Mom did I hear correctly; did she say six different places?"

"Yes you heard right son; Africa, China, Spain, Rome, India, and Egypt."

"The production manager of The Main Me asks for my appearance on one of the daily talk show spots. I'm also considering a special appearance on CPLS TV."

"My mama is a star," Byron boasts while bowing to Raimee.

"I need to give Acazia, Friend, and Mary the good news. I wonder if Mary has the same newfound fame. I'm calling her now."

∞

Mary answers, "Hi Raimee," and is abruptly interrupted by

Raimee saying, "Have you become famous? Do you have any voicemail messages?"

"Sorry girl, I didn't speak; how are you doing sweet Mary?"

Mary joyfully responds, "I'm doing good, and yes 43 messages were left with my mom. I'm gonna need voicemail," as she chuckles. "Mom will review them with me tomorrow. She tried to write down everything in the messages. Want to hear what was said?"

"Yes, let me hear."

"Mary Sutton, Tom Burns with WVTP. We want you for a commercial spot."

"The rest of the message is a phone number."

Raimee tries to give Mary guidance, "Make sure when you call to get all the details; let your mother and Bobby sit in. Promise me."

"I promise."

"A second message says, "Raimee, hold on, I want my family to hear this message also." Mary hustles to the living room. "Bobby, Malcolm, and mom listen to this message. Family, I also have Raimee on the phone. Mom, please give your opinion."

"Miss Mary Sutton how would you like an all expense paid trip for four to anywhere in the United States? Please call me, Jason Giltner as soon as you can to work out the details. Call 1-888-111-0092."

"Sis," Bobby exclaims, "You have to return the call to the message discussing people you can bring with you. Also find out the latest date you have to book any location and the latest date to go on any of the trips."

Excited Mary declares, "I feel so good now mom. Since I found Friend, my headaches are gone and I'm not confused any longer. I don't feel the need to run away from the neighborhood. No longer do I want to leave and just go anywhere else where no other person knows me. I'm happier."

∞

"Since I've been talking to Raimee and Friend I am deciding what I want to do with myself.

"I'm going to school and learn a skill, a trade; something that will pay more money so I can give more toward the bills and better help you with Bobby and Malcolm. Before, I didn't think I could accomplish much of anything. You know I could barely get up and go to work at the store. Now I know I can do a lot more. I have an appointment with the B&B Technical School.

"I want to thank GOD for sending me Friend, Raimee, and Acazia," Mary professes. "Since my return from Zenith, life has been so much better. I simply can't explain it, but it was worth the trip. I had no idea it would be so positive. Prior to meeting Friend, Acazia, and going to Zenith, I had feelings of doom. The whole world appears to practically change overnight, in a great way."

Ms. Sutton expresses her support, "Thank you baby for sharing. I'm glad you found something that gives you hope, purpose, and means this much to you."

"To show you how I have grown, I plan to go somewhere alone. I'm headed to the mall by myself and I'm not taking Sasha or you mom," Mary declares with pride in her step "This will be my first time ever shopping alone. I'm not nervous or anxious at all, and when I get back from shopping I'm going to take time and search for somewhere we all can go on a vacation."

∞

Talking to Mary on the phone, Raimee sits at her computer researching vacation destinations and looking at popular vacation spots in Africa and Egypt when her phone rings.

"Mary, I have a call coming through; I will call you tomorrow. Ms. Sutton, have a good night."

"Hello."

"Hi Raimee, it's Cordell Baisden. It has been a long time; how are you doing? I saw you on television but didn't know how to reach you. Do you know how long I have wanted to talk with you and to see you? When I saw you on TV, it felt like destiny. I continued until I found a way to contact you."

"Wow, it has been forever and out of the blue. What's up Cordell?"

"I know, I am just gonna put it out there." With fingers crossed, eyes kinda squinted, and lips twisted Cordell asks, "Will you go out with me to dinner and a movie?"

"I appreciate you, but I can't right now," Raimee answers. She is so glad he cannot see the expression on her face. "Thank you, I'll talk to you later."

"Okay, I'll call again another day. Stay sweet."

PERKS

Raimee picks up and answers the phone. "Hello, hi Mary, what are you doing?"

"How did you know it was me? Are you ready to go on our first shopping spree together?"

"Why not, somebody else is picking up the tab giving us unlimited spending and buying power."

"Where shall we go first?"

"How about we shop in order of location? We can hit as many places as possible. I don't think a limit was given on the number of stores or how much to spend."

Mary agrees, "Yeah we can hit all the ones in the same location before moving on to the next part of a town–it can save time."

"There are major department stores, high end stores, boutiques, and even stores that are not for fashion."

"I like department stores because of the variety of styles."

"I love boutiques, probably more than larger high end stores. One of the good things about boutiques versus department stores or bigger stores is more than likely you won't see a lot of the same styles."

"Why is that Raimee?"

"I like style, style that is unique. I have never really cared that much about labels and brand names. I truly like vintage style clothing and clothing from the 60's, 70's and 80's. I think I will like any and all the boutiques. You never know what you will find."

"That's so true."

Raimee continues, "We can shop regularly until our hearts are content by hitting as many stores as possible. There is no limit given on when we have to be finished with the shopping sprees. Let us shop on several different days. There is no way to get through a variety of boutiques, the mall, and several department stores in a couple of days.

"Our look can be different ways with the clothes and the makeup. There is glamorous, sheik, and sexy. Which one do you want to be?

"I want to be all. I can be one or two and my other me can be one or two. I will probably look sheik and glamorous. My other me will probably be sexy."

"Wait a minute, the other you. *What other you?"*

They both laugh.

"Let us research styles of clothing online for the glamorous, sheik, and sexy look. I am also interested in sophisticated. That's why I have another ME for when I feel like another person."

"I know how to research good on the net," Mary brags.

"That's good. I will let you do most of it. Okay?"

"Okay. Now we can take expensive trips, and bring our expensive clothes with us."

"Why carry clothes when we can buy new ones wherever we're going," Raimee expresses. "I want to go on a vacation and visit Africa, including Egypt, Ethiopia and Somalia, India, China, and France. I would like to go as soon as possible. While I'm taking extravagant vacations I'll buy some of those extravagant clothes."

"Promise me Raimee that we will take two trips together. Each of us will pick one."

"Mary, my friend, it will be especially nice. What a great idea."

"I've never been anywhere except the town I live in," Mary admits. "It will definitely be nice to go somewhere else. I want to go where it's warm, the waters are blue, it's peaceful, and I can feel comfortable. Somewhere my mom and two brothers will also like. It's a requirement family can go with me on the trips I choose. I'll need lodging, travel, and food for four."

"We received so many perks and opportunities. If it was not for Acazia, Friend, Xanthus, and all the Zenithians, we could not imagine doing any of this. All expense paid vacations, unlimited shopping sprees, cruises, the best parties and events with celebrities, FREE."

"That's what I'm talking about. Who gets chauffeured in a stretch limousine everywhere they go? We do," Mary says with such a happy and smiling face."

"I know what you mean, we are adored constantly, and our families are taken care of. We receive cars, college scholarship, and healthcare coverage taken care of. Healthcare coverage–not having to pay anything, no co-pay, no 20% out of pocket, not having to worry about being out of network in order to get the type of expertise that you need, and no deductibles to meet.

"Wow, my head is spinning just talking about it."

"My head is spinning just hearing you list all those money things," Mary proclaims with her hands held tightly and fingers gripping each other.

"It's a whole new life for me–so exciting, busy, and full of people wanting a piece of me, a piece of us. We went from nobody's and boredom to somebody's and stardom. It is unbelievable.

"How does it feel to you?"

"It's hard for me to believe too. It's all because of Zenith, Xanthus, Acazia, and Friend.

Raimee continues, "Okay, enough talk. It's time to get ready to hit the town."

"I don't have any idea of what to wear. What are you going to wear? We have all these gorgeous clothes and I just don't know what to do with them. I'm not used to being dressed up, especially in flashy stuff."

"Mary, because of the experience on Zenith I can be okay with this and any situation. I am much stronger now; I mean it. I feel so good about me in so many ways. I have never felt this good about myself, never this confident and alive being with me. Thanks GOD Xanthus, Acazia, Friend, and all the Zenithians who helped make *this me possible.*"

∞

Mary drives up and goes in the house, "Mom, Malcolm, and Bobby help me pick a vacation spot. I want to go somewhere for about two weeks on at least four trips. Each of us will select a destination for four. What do you think about that?"

Bobby gives Mary a big hug, "Oh Sis, I love it; I love you for wanting to include us."

"Thanks Sis," as Malcolm kisses Mary on the cheek.
Bobby and Malcolm begin researching vacation destination packages for the four of them.

Ms. Sutton professes, "Anywhere we go is fine with me darling. I just want to be with the three of you.

She suggests, "Although, all packages chosen will need to be all inclusive. All locations must include extensive spa and rejuvenation centers."

Bobby explains, "We will vacation in the US as our first. Later on we can try Hawaii."

"I can only imagine how beautiful Hawaiian vacations with its clear blue waters are," Mary declares.

APPEARANCES

T he requests for us to appear at various events keep rolling in. We can't keep up with them," Raimee explains. "Maybe we can make separate guest appearances."

"Okay, I'm sure I can do it."

"Alright Mary, I'm listing the events, dates, and which one of us will be the guest. We can discuss the details of each. Let us have a weekly meeting to work out the specifics. We'll meet the first time on January 21st at 2 pm."

April 5	Raimee and Mary, same venue
April 14	Mary
April 22	Raimee and Mary - different venues
April 29	Mary and Raimee - different venues
May 3	Raimee
May 12	Raimee and Mary, same venue
May 17	Mary
May 26	Raimee and Mary - different venues
June 7	Mary
June 15	Raimee and Mary - different venues
June 20	Mary and Raimee - same venue
June 27	Raimee

"This list is for April thru June. Requests are in through the rest of the year. We will continue weekly meetings. Other events may come up between now and some of the dates listed. Keep our finger crossed. Scheduled dates will be adjusted only if absolutely necessary, although, the goal is as much as possible to keep dates at the original schedule."

∞

Raimee's co-workers start acting as if she is special.

Raimee's co-worker Camille approaches her the next day at work and says. "Raimee, what's up with you girl? What are you doing this weekend? Let's go to the casino."

Is she asking me to do something with her? Wow, I feel privileged.

∞

The next day while meeting, Raimee asked Lakeeda and Sasha, "How were the voices communicating? I do not understand the reasoning behind the headaches and voices in my head helping you to communicate with me. I did not understand any of what the voices were saying.

"So how was that communicating? Please explain it to me."

"I want to understand the reason also," Mary appeals.

Lakeeda professes, "That *is* a fair question Raimee and Mary. I do not have a long detailed explanation. We had to find a way to communicate and to make a physical connection. The only way we could initially inhabit your mind and body was to connect via voices inside. Connecting with your mind allowed us the ability to transmit and receive audio and visual insight into what was going on with you, and how the society you live in affects you.

"The voices were distressing to you and I am sorry for that but this was the only way we could inhabit, undetected, until we entered your daily lives for the awakening you were to receive as the chosen EBOI's. It assisted getting us to the point where we are with both of you. It helped get you to the point of truly being ready for your Earthly rebirth."

∞

Mary strolls through the neighborhood once foreign to her. She is now comfortable talking to others without the physical, mental, and emotional negativity previously affecting her. There are no specific memories of mistreatment from others, personal and work environments. She is more confident and alive.

Raimee is now assertive in her personal and professional life. Her confidence and self-esteem has shot through the roof. It appears everything she touches turns to gold. She proudly says, "I'm living my best life."

AUTHOR BIO

ARIES ZENREAL lives in the Appalachian mountains of West Virginia.

Her many thoughts she shares through captured stories from a touch of experience and a lot of imagination.

When not putting pen to paper she enjoys her family and her cats.